OBSESSION

The Quinn Larson Quests

P.A. WILSON

FREE EBOOK

Claim your copy of Spells and Other Charms when you use the QR code to sign up for my newsletter and learn more about Quinn and Cate's past.

It was Saturday, and it was going to be Dionne's first full day with us. Lionel was up early. By the smell of bleach and vinegar, he must have cleaned the house before I got up. As soon as I had my breakfast in front of me, he said, "I'm going for groceries. If Dionne's going to be here all day, we can't expect her to live off tea and oatmeal."

I dug into the pocket of my jeans for money and handed him a wad of bills. As his footsteps echoed from the hall, I realized I'd need to generate more income if I was going to be supporting two teenagers. Just another detail in the complexity of my new life. I made most of my money through on-line ads that I'd set up before I lost my sight. I'd been surprised how easy it was to lace a spell through the internet. I never compelled people to buy, just to click. That's all it took to keep enough money going to my account to pay the bills. And it didn't take much power from me to keep the spell running.

The problem wasn't really the money. No matter how much I tried to ignore it, the real problem was Dionne. I'd never trained a witch before, other wizards trained witches and wizards alike. My only experience was Lionel, and I'd inherited him from Cate. On top of that, Dionne was one of the six wizards with five powers who would bring about a prophecy that no one seemed to understand.

As if that wasn't bad enough, she'd grown up among the humans and didn't know she was a witch until we tested her.

"Hello, Quinn?" Dionne called from the door. "Are you there?"

I realized that in the rush after her test I hadn't given her access through the wards. "Come in, I'm in the kitchen." That would give her access to the main floor. Later, I could put some layers on the workshop to restrict her in the same way Lionel wasn't able to access everything down there.

While she came down the hall, I added a quiet restriction to stop her from inviting people in without Lionel or me present. I didn't want to come home one day to find a party raging in the living room.

She plunked down in the chair next to mine. "I'm yours until eight. I couldn't get the foster parents to buy that I'd be cleaning a river after dark. I told them I was having dinner with friends. We should probably introduce Lionel as my friend soon. How are you?"

I laughed. This was going to be interesting, not easy, but definitely interesting. "I'm fine. Lionel will be back in a few minutes. Make yourself comfortable."

"No. I'm good," she said. "Listen, I had an idea last night. Maybe you can pretend to be my uncle. If you did, I would be able to move in here. Then everything would be better."

I heard Lionel come in as I tried to marshal an argument. From a learning point of view, it would be much better if she was living here. From a peace of mind point of view, I wasn't sure I was ready to have a chattering teenage girl around all the time. And purely logistically, there wasn't a free bedroom. We'd have to clear a room in the attic, and I wasn't able to do the renovation spell it would require because I couldn't see. And I didn't know if I should trust Lionel with it. "Wouldn't the authorities need a lot of proof before handing you over to an uncle?" I asked, hoping human bureaucracy would come to my rescue.

"Yeah there would be paperwork, but we could make it right with magic. We could use a spell to convince them." She'd obviously been giving this a lot of thought. My guess was she'd been wishing for an uncle or aunt to show up for years.

I hated to flatten her hopes, but I didn't need the intrusion of whatever government agency looked after foster children. "I don't think that's a good idea because there's probably a lot of checks and balances. It would be a very complex spell. And—"

"But we could do it." She trampled over my words.

"We could at least try to find out," Lionel chipped in. "It would be better for her to get full time training. I mean it's going to take months just to get her to understand the world we live in."

"See, Lionel agrees with me," Dionne said.

I shook my head. "Nice try. He doesn't agree with you, but he has a point. We'll see what it would take. But I need to know a lot more about your parents first. If I'm an uncle, I should be able to tell someone about them. I don't even know what they looked like."

"There are pictures you can look at." Her voice was suddenly quiet.

"You have pictures?" That would go a long way to helping solve the mystery of who she was, but Lionel would have to be my eyes, as usual.

I heard a little catch in her breath before she spoke again. "No, I don't. The pictures are of the crime scene. The police have them. I can get them if you like, but I don't think I can look at them."

I didn't need my sight to know she was fighting tears.

I wanted to pat her shoulder but wasn't willing to take the chance of what I would end up touching. "We'll start by figuring out how to get the files from the police. Then we'll talk about moving you here. But right now, we need to put you under a new glamour."

"Why?" Her interest was back, and I let myself believe I'd dodged the bullet of her living arrangements for now.

"We're going to take you to Banks' pub for lunch," Lionel said.

"I'm too young to go to a pub," she said.

"You can go into this one. No one will be the wiser, at least no human. Real folk don't care how old you are as long as you don't disturb the relative peace. Even so, you'll be drinking tea or coffee. I'm not sending you back to your foster parents with alcohol on your breath." I paused to let her react, but she didn't say anything, so I continued, "The glamour will change your appearance slightly. Just enough so no one will recognize you. The Real Folk will notice your appearance has been altered, but everyone occasionally adds or subtracts a bit from their looks. No one will be suspicious."

"Cool," she said. "Will it be enough to stop people who know me really well recognizing me? Like I would hate to have someone tell the foster parents they saw me downtown when I was supposed to be in Richmond."

I was going to have to break her of the habit of adding 'like' into her conversations. Preciseness of language was a vital component of successful spell casting. "Yes, it will hide you from people you know."

"Can I be a redhead? A tall redhead? I've always wanted to be tall and glamorous."

I nodded and directed her down to the workroom. "Lionel will do the glamour. It will be good practice for him. And while he does, I'll start your lessons with the history of the world."

I heard a groan from both of them. Lionel was still struggling to get his glamours right, despite his success with Beacon, and Dionne was probably expecting a dry list of battles and knights. I suppressed a chuckle. "When I'm satisfied your glamour is complete, Lionel, we'll go. I have a mirror down here somewhere that Dionne can look in to see what you've done."

It took two hours for Lionel to get the look Dionne wanted, because she kept asking for just a little more, and I wouldn't step in to say no. I could feel the power of the spell settle and it would be enough to deflect any Real Folk from looking too deeply and seeing her powers. My quick summary of the world as we know it had grabbed Dionne's interest and I was encouraged to think she'd be as good a student as Lionel.

We left to go to Banks' for lunch, and I was looking forward to her reaction to the full gamut of Real Folk.

WE STAYED FOR LUNCH AND ENOUGH TIME FOR LIONEL AND ME to enjoy a couple of beers while Dionne did her best to sound cool without missing anything that was going on. She'd been chattering all the way back to the house. "That was cool, can we go back? I want to talk to everyone again." She was buzzing with energy.

I released some of the wards on my workroom and waved her ahead of me. "Yes, but we need to spend some time on your training."

She kept up a running commentary as we made our way down the few steps and across to the center of the bare earth. Lesson learned for me, never start the day with a trip to Banks'.

I heard the door close and Lionel clomp down to join us. "Wait until you see it on a busy day," he said. "You didn't even get to meet any kobolds or sidhe. That was weird, Quinn. I wonder why the sidhe weren't there."

I felt really old compared to with the energy radiating off the two of them. "I don't know, Lionel. Before we worry about that, how about we give Dionne some more of the history of the Real Folk?"

"Great idea," Lionel said.

Dionne groaned. "Can't we just start with some spells? If there's a history book, I can take it home and read it. Or if we have to do research, why not start with my prophecy?"

I ignored the whine building in her voice. "Spells will come later. Unless you want to just stay here for lessons and not meet other people? Not go to Banks'? We'll get to the prophecy soon."

"Why not now?"

I could almost feel the pout that must be on her face. "I need to figure out how to approach the investigation. It's complicated, Dionne."

"Okay, fine. But does it have to be all the history? Like, can we just go over the high points? Then maybe some spells?" She paused. "Or, maybe you can tell me what you know about the prophecy. Maybe that will give us a clue how to start."

It was a reasonable question. I just didn't have any information for her. "We'll start with some history. If we have time, I'll talk about the prophecy." And maybe I would have some idea what to say when we got to it.

"Yes, we have to think about what we know," Lionel said. "I have to warn you, Dionne, there isn't much information."

She sighed, and I held back a wince. I'd broken Lionel of that habit, and now I would have to start again. "Okay, no problem," she said, bouncing back with all the energy of a teenager. "So, am I going to have to memorize a bunch of dates? Battles and stuff?"

I laughed. "No, it's more about the stories of the Real Folk, the magical people. How they arrived here, their power, their weaknesses. And the threat they pose."

"You'll like it. Like Quinn said, it's stories." Lionel put something on the bench and added, "Shall I make tea?"

We'd already burned half the day at Banks' and needed to get on with the lessons. "Maybe later. A couple of hours of history and then we'll have a break."

"Why do we have to work down here?" Dionne asked from

somewhere near the window. "It would be more comfortable upstairs. And there'll be more light."

"Yes, but it's more private down here." I pointed toward where the couch had been last time. "Have a seat."

Her footsteps stopped. "Why do we need privacy?" There was fear in her voice. Something that I hadn't heard in all the times we'd talked before. She'd always been in control, even when she'd met us in the park.

"I want Lionel to cast some images for you," I said. "Why are you worried?"

"I'm not. So, let's get on with it."

I decided to let it go. She would tell me eventually. "Okay, let's get settled."

I had Lionel create images of the kobolds to start with, and then told him to explain their powers and weaknesses. I had learned the value of getting two things done at the same time when I first took on Lionel as an apprentice.

After Lionel had recited the kobold descriptions, I said, "The sidhe are more complicated, but Lionel can give you the run down on the structure of the court, and then we'll put off the rest until later."

"Quinn," Lionel said. "I've been thinking. Maybe we should look at the facts we know about the prophecy."

Didn't either of them understand the relationship between master and apprentice? I was going to have to work hard to stay in control.

"Yeah, that would be good," Dionne said. "I can learn this other stuff later."

"Let's see how well you learned the kobolds before we stop the lessons." I sympathized with her. She had been living a lie all of her life. I could sympathize with Lionel too. This was all stuff he knew. Bringing Dionne into her birthright shouldn't stall his training, but it would. All I could do was let him teach as much as possible, at least that would reinforce his training.

It was time to start the quiz. "Dionne, name three characteristics of the kobold that points to their heritage."

Another sigh introduced the answer. "They are armored. This shows they developed in a place that could have caused them damage. They are strong, meaning their environment was harsh. They are capable of disguising themselves, meaning they lived, or traveled, among humans."

She had done a good job of synthesizing the facts that Lionel had given her. "You have a good memory. I think we can limit ourselves to a couple of species a visit."

"So, we can talk about the prophecy?"

"No," I said. Hearing two people take in a breath to argue, I held up my hand. "Just listen. Lionel and I need to do more research before we talk about it. I promise we won't keep anything from you."

"I can do some research tonight," Lionel said.

"Can I help?" Dionne asked. "I'm good at research. I always get great marks on my projects."

I'd talk to Lionel later to get him to slow down and maybe get him to take my side in these situations. He needed to help get Dionne trained before we let her get into prophecies. "Let's move onto sprite folklore and then we'll break for a snack."

We were gathered at the counter, tea and blueberry scones fortifying us, for the next part of the lessons. I was going to teach Dionne to boil water. Well, Lionel would teach her with me listening to the instructions.

The doorbell rang as I was explaining the theory of the spell. "Lionel, go see who that is. Dionne, please go into my bedroom until we know it's safe." The last thing we needed was for someone to find one of the six before she was ready.

Dionne took her tea and pastry with her.

The bell rang again before Lionel got to it. I heard a high piping voice and Lionel's rumble. Princess – Great! The bringer of many problems.

I knew Lionel would limit her access to the house, but she was sneaky. I would have to trust him to keep an eye on her while she visited. I waited until they joined me before acknowledging her. "Princess, it's a delight to have you in my home."

"I know, Quinn Larson." She touched my hand and I felt the dryness of her skin. Princess was getting old. "You still cannot see, is that correct?"

"I have not found the cure for Fionuir's spell, no."

"Then I must tell you that I have brought my eldest daughter with me today. I must ask you for a favor."

"What do you need from me?"

"First, let me introduce my child. Quinn Larson, this is Bud, my child and heir. She will rule the Rose tribe when I am gone."

"A long time from now I hope?" I held out a hand low to the ground. "It is good to meet you, Bud." I felt the touch of tiny fingers.

"I've never met a wizard before. How do you cast spells if you can't see?" Bud's voice was barely audible it was so high in pitch.

"I manage. Can I offer you anything? Perhaps some honey?" I had lost track of Lionel. I hoped he was monitoring Princess. The last time she came to ask for a favor, or told me she would do me a favor by allowing me to find her treasure, she'd tried to drop enough beads in my house to grant her access regardless of my wards.

"I do not have time today for your hospitality," Princess said. "I need you to train Bud to be a leader."

"What makes you think I could do that? I have little knowledge of fairy politics." And I really didn't have time to train anyone else.

Princess gave a sigh that rivaled Dionne's efforts. I was going to have to cast a no sighing spell on the house before it drove me mad.

"See mother, I told you I didn't need training."

"Bud, be quiet. I know what you need. I am the queen, and you will obey me." Princess snapped her fingers. "Now, Quinn Larson, it is not lessons in politics I ask for. She is lacking in compassion. I worry that she will become a poor leader."

I couldn't bring Bud into my house. Dionne needed me more than Princess, and too many people around meant too big a chance her secret would come out. "There are other people who can do a much better job at teaching her than I can."

"No. You are the best teacher. Lionel is a much better wizard, and man, than he was. You have taken time to teach him more than magic."

I should know better than to try to argue with Princess. I hadn't won an argument yet, but I had to try. "I didn't want an apprentice, Princess, you know that. I only took him on because I owed Cate. I'm not taking on another one."

"I hear you have already taken on another. This girl you brought into Banks' this morning. Dionne, is that her name?"

Damn. "Yes, that's her name. So, you can see, for a wizard who wanted no apprentices, I have enough to keep me busy."

"Bud is small. She will not take up much of your time." Princess was not going to let me off the hook. "If you train her well, you will not have to help the fairies again, perhaps."

"That's a big perhaps, Princess. Have you done something to my apprentice?"

"He is held at the door by a charm. I will free him when I leave. I did not wish him to witness my embarrassment." Her voice didn't carry any tinge of embarrassment. She'd frozen Lionel to show me she still had the power; or maybe to prove it to herself.

It was time to try another tack. "If I were to agree, there would be conditions." There had to be something she wouldn't agree to.

"I expected as much. Tell me them so we can be done. I am tiring."

I thought for a moment. If I lost the negotiation, there was one thing I needed in place to ensure Dionne's safety. "I need her to take the apprentice oath. I have things I do not wish made public."

"I can keep secrets," Bud squeaked from behind me.

Princess hissed. "I said to be quiet. You see what I must put up with, Quinn Larson. She will take your vow. What else?"

This was too easy. "She will be here at nine every day and will do as we ask. She will take orders from me, and my apprentices, without argument."

Princess laughed, a rising tinkle of sound that ended in a gasp for air. She was really coming to the end of her life. "If you can get her to agree to the last part of that, you truly are a great teacher. I will ensure she is here on time. Is there anything else?"

I conceded. "No, we'll start tomorrow."

I felt a touch on my hand. "Thank you, Quinn. This is the most important favor you have done for me. Until tomorrow."

"Tomorrow. Don't forget to release Lionel."

She laughed again. "Your lack of sight is not a problem for your memory, I see. I will not forget to release him, and he will not be hurt. You will need him when my child comes for her lessons." She patted my hand. "Bud, come along. Tomorrow you can take your oath."

"Princess, be well. I would not like to lose you before Bud is trained."

A featherlike kiss landed on my cheek. "I would not let that happen to my tribe."

A few seconds later, Lionel stomped back into the kitchen. "I heard everything. You are getting a reputation for teaching, Quinn. Maybe we should look into those renovations. Maybe we can turn the attic into bedrooms and open a school. This is so cool."

"Let's get back to teaching Dionne while we only have her to worry about." I called the girl back to the kitchen.

BY THE TIME WE'D FINISHED OUR SNACK, DIONNE HAD THE theory for the water boiling spell down pat. We were just getting ready to head down to the workroom when the doorbell rang again.

"We are popular today," I said gesturing to Dionne to go back into my bedroom. "We'll both go to the door this time, Lionel. You stand back with a repel spell just in case someone tries the same thing as Princess did. We can't be spending time waiting for freeze spells to pass." I heard my bedroom door close and turned to the front hall.

"Quinn, let me look through the peephole. No one can cast through the house wards. When we know who's there, we can be better prepared."

I gave him a little push so he was ahead of me. I was so used to my blindness that I sometimes forgot I couldn't do everything I used to. "Don't open the door until I tell you."

It felt a bit like we were defending my house from attackers. But if Princess was able to cast a spell on my apprentice, I wasn't willing to chance what a stranger would do.

"It's three druids," Lionel said in awe.

Druids; this day was not getting better. "Okay, let them in with restrictions to this floor." I started back to the living room. I might as well get comfortable.

I heard Lionel chatting, but the druids didn't speak to him. I couldn't understand why he seemed to revere them when they ignored him.

"Quinn Larson," a dry voice announced.

"Yes." I wasn't going to give them any help.

"You have done us a service in the past. We require you to do one more thing." The voice came from beside me, this time. I was used to that. All druids either sounded the same, or made themselves sound that way, to outsiders.

"You require? I have no obligation to you."

"We will not accept denial of our request."

"Requests do not come as requirements." I didn't know how badly they wanted this thing, but I wanted time to train my apprentices in peace. If insulting them would make the druids go away, I'd take the chance.

There was a dry rustle of whispers. Then they turned their

attention back to me. "Perhaps our choice of words was unfortunate. We have a problem and believe you are the solution."

I felt Lionel settle beside me on the couch. The druids had promised to teach him when he was ready, and he knew better than to risk their goodwill. If he kept silent, he wouldn't put that in jeopardy no matter what I said or did.

"What is your problem?"

"Then you agree to do us this service?"

"No, I am curious to know what you need. I may choose to help if you are willing to negotiate for my time."

"You must free the sidhe Fionuir from the dimensional fold in which you have her prisoner."

That was a surprise. I knew Fionuir would have to be freed eventually. I wasn't stupid enough to think I could keep her there forever. I had hoped it would be done by someone else long after I was gone. And if I had to release her before that, I would need a lot of protection. "I'll ignore your choice of words. Why do you need her freed?"

"Why is not important. We require this of you."

I reminded myself that patience is a virtue, and that the druids would never change their demanding approach. They would tell me what I needed to know if they wanted to, and if I asked the right questions. "I do not wish to obstruct your plans but releasing her is not my sole discretion. I believe Queen Maeve will want some power in that decision. And there are others who Fionuir may feel compelled to punish for her imprisonment. I am happy to carry your message, but I need to know why you wish her freed. If I know that, I can plead your case."

There were whispers for a few minutes before the druid on my left spoke again. "We are also constrained by other concerns, which we do not wish to share with you."

"I will keep your secrets. I cannot convince Queen Maeve without information." Maybe a reminder of her stature would help them bend.

"We cannot simply provide information. Before we consider sharing more, tell us if it is possible to release Fionuir."

"Yes, I can bring her back to this dimension. I have created alternate avenues for doing so in the event I am unable." Clarence had one spelled charm and Olan the other. Neither would use them unless they knew I was dead. "Before you ask, I will not tell you what those alternate avenues are."

"It is not important. Signs point to you as the person who imprisoned her. You must be the one to free her."

"What signs?" I was just about done with their secrecy.

There was whispering again, and then the voice came from my right this time, "The souls in the Gur amulet are stirring."

That wasn't good. The Gur amulet contained the souls of murdered druids. If they were stirring... well it wouldn't be good news. "What makes you think that has anything to do with Fionuir?"

"We cannot say, but we will ask the council if we can share any information. It would be helpful to give them assurance that you will free her. It is important that the souls remain at rest. Even Queen Maeve will not be happy with the results if they should be more disturbed."

"I cannot give you those assurances without conditions." I was beyond tired of this. We were wasting the little time we had of Dionne's day. There was nothing in my bedroom to teach her, but there was no way I was letting her out in front of the druids. I'd keep her secret from them as long as possible. If they knew they had access to one of the six, they wouldn't leave her alone, and we would be overrun with creepy guys in black robes and hoods. My neighbors would start to suspect I was not normal – for a human anyway.

The rustling stopped. A voice came from the far side of the room. "Name your conditions."

I felt Lionel shifting on the couch beside me and figured he wanted me to include some more training time with the druids. I ignored the command in the voice. "I must have Maeve's approval. Fionuir is her subject, and I am not interfering with sidhe politics."

"It seems you have already done that by imprisoning Fionuir," a dry voice said. "Or perhaps you were acting on Maeve's orders?"

I wasn't going to gossip about the sidhe Queen. "Maeve did not order me to get rid of Fionuir." Well, not actually, but she wasn't unhappy about it when I sent her rival away.

"Very well, are there any other conditions you wish to place on the peace of our murdered brothers' souls?"

"No more conditions, but I will require compensation. I will be taking a risk by freeing her. Fionuir will not be happy about her imprisonment." That was an understatement. She'd make my life a living hell, and I'd be lucky if she didn't kill me.

"We cannot agree to payment, but we will take your price to the council. I would not ask for too much, wizard."

I'm not sure why they didn't come prepared. Did they assume I would just agree to the request to free her? "You owe Lionel a month of training. I would have that extended to two months. In addition, I have need of information."

"We hold much knowledge in our library. Anyone is welcome to research any topic they desire while in there."

That was true, but nothing was indexed. Or more accurately the index wasn't made available to non-druids, and there was a magic dampening spell cast across the whole building. "I do not wish to spend my life trying to find the information I seek. The price, if I agree to release her, is to receive the information directly."

"Perhaps the council will agree to that. What is this information?"

"I will tell you that when we have an agreement. Now, I have an apprentice to train. Is there anything else we need to discuss before you can speak to your council?"

I heard a rustle of fabric and felt Lionel rise. "We will return after speaking to the council. Be prepared to act when we next meet. You will get approval from Maeve while you wait for the council's decision."

"Yes, I think it's best that we deal with this as quickly as possible." Their attitude had pushed my courtesy to the edge. "Perhaps it is time for you to do your part."

Lionel showed them out, and by the time he got back, Dionne was in the kitchen. "If I have to keep hiding in there every time someone comes over, can you keep something interesting for me to do? Like, your computer or something?"

"I hope we won't be interrupted again today, but that's a good idea. Lionel can sort out some history books for you to study." The groan I heard did not surprise me. "Let's get you working on the water spell before you have to leave."

DIONNE MANAGED TO GET SOME STEAM RISING FROM A VERY small cup of water before she left. I had expected her to be frustrated at the slow progress, but she was cheerful with what she had accomplished. We were still working out her schedule, but she promised to try to come by for at least part of the day tomorrow. I worried that if we couldn't work full days on weekends, we'd be forever getting her trained.

Now, Lionel was digging through some of my older texts for hints about the prophecy, and I fully expected he would be there all night. It was getting close to midnight and my mind was restless with the day's events. I made a mug of calming tea and went to the back garden to attempt to sort everything out.

It was still warm enough in the evenings to enjoy the night air. I maintained a spell over the house, and my neighbors to keep the mosquitoes at bay, so it was always comfortable in the garden. I sank back in one of the wicker chairs and imagined the night sky. The moon would be almost full but hidden behind the towers a few blocks away.

One of my neighbors was still up, a faint murmur of music drifting across the lane. The gentle noise was better for my mood than silence would have been. I sent my senses out further, hearing the whisper of traffic on Burrard Street. A sudden scream of an ambulance siren startled me back to myself. Living so close to St. Paul's hospital was the only downside of the neighborhood.

I sipped the tea and felt the calm from the herbs flow through my body. A deep breath took my cares out on the exhale. Things would work out. Having Bud in the house would help Dionne, who was feeling the gap between Lionel's knowledge and her own. Although she hadn't mentioned it, I could feel it in every sigh and silence.

If the druids met my conditions, and Maeve could contain her, I'd be happy to free Fionuir. I knew we had no choice but to put her there when she attacked us. I didn't like to leave her in the dimensional fold. People went mad in such isolation.

"Quinn, are you not aware of me? Or are you ignoring me?" The voice was warm, and soft, and welcoming.

I spilled tea on my lap. "Damn, how did you get there without me noticing?"

"Language, Quinn," The Morrigan said, her voice now more like a crow and carrying a clear warning.

"Sorry, you startled me. It is good to see you, so to speak."

I felt warm flesh press against my arm. Even without sight, I felt the raw sexuality of her fertility aspect. It became hard to breathe, and then the flesh turned into feathers, and the chill of death replaced the heat of sex. I wanted to ask her to stay in crow form, it was less distracting, but I'd already crossed a line, so I kept my mouth shut.

"I forgive you, this time."

"Is this a social visit?"

"It is not. I have come to warn you. The thing I have been sensing is approaching. Something is changing the fate of this world."

Despite the fact I could feel her warm skin against my arm again, she sounded angry enough to peck my eyes out.

So much for the idea of relaxing before I went to bed. I'd thought she was omniscient. It was disconcerting to think that there was something that she could only sense. "Do you have any idea what it is?"

I heard a caw and felt the life drain from me. "No, I do not!" She switched back to woman and life flowed back into my body on a warm silky breeze. "It is not usual that something should be hidden from me. It is normal for me to choose what to tell and what to keep hidden. I am not happy about this situation, Quinn Larson."

I didn't know what to say. How did one comfort the goddess of death and life? "I'm sure you will know before any of us."

A beak clacked. "It doesn't matter. I will feed on the aftermath either way."

I was weary of the tension that long encounters with The Morrigan brought. Not knowing whether I would be filled with grief or lust – and getting both – frayed my nerves. "Is there something I can do for you?" I hoped not. I had enough on my plate.

"Yes." The warmth of my first love flowed with the word. "Be careful. I think this thing is aimed at you. Or perhaps someone close to you."

"You care about me?" Was that a good thing?

"I care about all creatures. I am there at their creation and at their destruction." The pain of birth and battle death filled my mind. "But yes, Quinn, you interest me. I am not ready to take your spirit, yet."

A flap of wings and an icy breeze stopped my next question. She was gone. The night warmed and the scent of jasmine from my garden replaced a whiff of death.

The next morning, Lionel and I were in the workroom early. He'd had no luck finding new information. If there was anything in my library that would shed light on Dionne's future, it was hidden behind a subtle spell. It was time to take another approach.

"The circle is finished," Lionel said. "The candy is ready when you are."

Spirits liked bribes. Candy was easy to get, and popular, so we'd start with that, and if we got no response, we'd move on to the alcohol. The only problem with alcohol was it could attract a lot of spirits with a thirst for booze and no information.

"When you put out the call, be specific about the question; exactly as we rehearsed." I wasn't as comfortable with it as I pretended to be. Lionel needed practice on spirit work, so I was letting him run the summoning. "Talk me through it one more time before you start."

"I put the candy in the center and light the incense. I say the question into the smoke."

"That's right. Do you want to start with the amulet questions, or the prophecy?" As I said it, I realized how much was on my shoulders. The prophecy was probably slightly less critical. The druids weren't going to be asking about that later today.

"The amulet. I don't like the idea that those souls are stirring. I always kind of pictured them sleeping. It must be horrible to be trapped in there."

I nodded to him to start and heard the scritch of a match being run across stone. The odor of sulfur filled the room, followed by sandalwood.

"We are calling for information on the souls in the Gur amulet. Why are they stirring?" His words were accompanied by the squeak of candy wrappers being opened.

I waited, hoping we would hear quickly. The spirit world runs on a different time than ours, so sometimes it takes hours for a response.

"Quinn Larson's apprentice," a voice like a winter storm roared through the circle. "I will have your name."

I held up a hand. Ranseed wasn't a demon you could practice on. Especially anyone connected to me. We had a misunderstanding years ago, that he refused to get over. "Do you have information for us, Ranseed?"

"I have information," he hissed.

That could mean anything. I wasn't going to be that easily tricked. "Is it of value to us?" His answer was a howl of frustration that bruised my ears. "If you have nothing for us, don't expect payment."

"My information is of value to you, but I do not guarantee you will see the value now." Ranseed had regained control of his temper. "The name of your apprentice will be payment enough."

I raised an eyebrow. It was up to Lionel. Giving his name didn't mean he was giving power to Ranseed, but it meant the spirit would have a way to pretend they had a relationship. That could build power over the years. I would have to give Lionel some skills on avoiding these pitfalls when we were done.

"My name is Lionel."

"I need your full name, apprentice," Ranseed shrieked.

"I have no other name," Lionel said.

I kept my mind blank, and my mouth shut. If Ranseed didn't believe Lionel, there was nothing I could do. It wasn't unusual for wizards to have only one name. Most of them earned other names as they grew.

"Very well, Lionel of the one name, I accept the payment," Ranseed said. I felt a slight shift of power as he accepted the name.

"What is your information?" Lionel asked.

"The souls are stirring. We feel it in the spirit world because they are partly in your world and partly in another. As long as they remain in the amulet, they will stay that way."

I waited for Lionel to keep going. It was his spell, and I needed to let him run it. Ranseed hadn't tried anything sneaky, yet. I stayed alert to the possibility of trickery anyway.

"Do you know why?" Lionel pressed.

"It is not safe for you to ask these questions. I do not give advice usually, but I like you Lionel one name. Do not pry further into druid business."

Lionel didn't answer. A good tactic if Ranseed was holding out. The time stretched out until I was ready to step in. Then suddenly the air sucked out of the room. I was gasping to bring oxygen into my lungs for what felt like an eternity before it rushed back tasting of ice and honey.

"You must release me," Ranseed whined. "I have given you what I know."

Lionel had paid the price, so it was in his power to hold Ranseed. I wouldn't let him get into trouble, but I was interested in what he was doing.

"I will release you, but I am not satisfied with your information. I gave you my name. You gave us a warning instead of information. If you have nothing else to say on the Gur souls, I would take information on the prophecy of the six."

Maybe Lionel could teach me a few things about negotiating. I would have released Ranseed and tried another source.

"There is little known about that prophecy," Ranseed said. "Change will come when the six meet in the same age."

"I knew that much. If you have no other actual information, do you know where I should look?"

"Why, Lionel one name? Why are you interested in the prophecy of the six?"

I heard him sigh before he answered, "Quinn has assigned me the task of researching obscure prophecies. I was hoping you could save me some time."

"You will find more wisdom in the search, apprentice Lionel." Ranseed laughed. It was the sound of a sandstorm. "I have no information for you, but I have confidence that you will find what you seek."

"I release you," Lionel said.

Ranseed didn't say goodbye. The room simply became fresh.

"Clear the spell," I said. "I think we've done enough for the morning."

Lionel said the clearing spell to dismiss any lingering spirits then extinguished the incense. "The circle is clean. I'm sorry we didn't learn anything. Maybe we should try again later?"

"You handled him well. I think we should wait until the druids return before digging into this any further."

I tried to tell myself that I wasn't a coward, but I didn't believe it. This prophecy, along with the demand to release Fionuir, and the warning I got when I tried to find out what happened to Dionne's parents, were adding up to something to be scared of.

"I think we need to talk about next week," I said following Lionel up the stairs. "I'm going to need some help with Bud and Dionne."

I heard him click the lock on the workroom door right after I stepped through. It was a good idea to be extra vigilant now that we'd have a full house.

"Quinn, maybe I can help with Dionne. I don't need as much training, so I could do the basics with her while you focus on Bud."

He wasn't ready to be a teacher yet, but he had a point. "I am not going to ignore your needs. And Bud isn't going to learn from lectures. We'll work out something. What time is it?"

"Ten. Tea?"

The sound of water filling the kettle made me thirsty. "Yes, please. I was expecting Bud by now. This isn't a good start."

He turned off the tap and clanked the kettle on the stove. "Maybe Princess thought this was a Monday to Friday kind of thing. Or maybe she's too sick to get here today."

"What do you mean?" Princess hadn't sounded sick, just tired.

"She was almost transparent. I don't know if it was just age, or if she was sick. Remember when she first came to you? When she hadn't eaten for days?"

I did. It was before my sight was taken, before Fionuir had lost her fight to keep the sidhe throne, before I sent her away with the book that held the spell to heal my sight in her pocket. "Yes, she looked faded, like a rose that needed sunshine."

"This time she looked like she was disappearing. I checked last night... in that book... *Lives of the Real Folk*. I think she's only going to live a few more days, maybe a week."

Fairies burned brightly and then went out in a blink. I realized that Princess was probably halfway through her life when I first met her. "We need to work fast with Bud. If she doesn't show up tomorrow by nine fifteen, you'll need to go out and get her."

"Quinn, can I come in?" Dionne called from the front door.

"You don't have to ask," I called back. "Lionel, is there enough hot water for a third cup of tea?"

"I don't need any. I can't stay long. The foster parents are expecting me back soon," Dionne said. "I just wanted to tell you that we're good for after school. I can spend a couple of hours here every day."

"Slow down," I said patting the stool beside me. "Why are your foster parents okay with you coming here?" I swallowed the fear that they knew about us. Dionne couldn't tell them about the Real Folk because of her oath, but that didn't mean they couldn't figure it out. Then again, why would humans figure that out?

"I told them I have an after-school job. They were impressed." There was a hint of regret in her voice. She cared what they thought more than she was willing to admit. "It would help if you can give me some money. Like a paycheck?"

"What do they think you are doing?" Lionel asked.

"Office work. So, about the pay, it doesn't need to be much."

So much for the day getting less complicated. "What about the weekend? You won't progress fast enough in a few hours a day."

I heard her start to sigh then catch herself. "On the weekends they think I'm doing volunteer work. It will help me get into University. If you won't let me move in, that's the best I can do."

"Should I be worried that you can lie so easily?"

I heard a chuckle. "It's not really lying, Quinn. I could tell them the truth and see how well that works."

"Quinn, I think Dionne probably knows the difference between a real lie and something that can't be avoided."

It was so unusual to have a witch who grew up with humans. Normally lying was strictly banned between a master and apprentice, because too many things could get completely disastrous if the master wasn't clear on what the apprentice was up to. Then again, normally apprentices found ways around it. I had with very little effort.

"I know I'm probably being paranoid, but if your foster parents get suspicious, they could cause problems. As for paying you, I don't want to get into paperwork, Dionne." The last thing we needed was humans poking around while we tried to seem normal.

"That should be okay. It's not like the foster parents are going to ask for pay stubs. They are just happy I have a job."

"How much? I don't have a lot of cash coming in. The Real Folk don't have much use for it." I just generated enough from my website to pay for groceries and taxes.

"Can you do fifty bucks a week? That's what my friends make from their part time work."

I would have to trust her on that. "I can probably manage that. I'll have to tweak my affiliate site."

"You make money on-line? Cool. I can help you with that, too. Maybe I can try to come back later and set you up with some cool links."

I felt her rise. "I don't need to make a lot of money, Dionne, but thanks for offering to help. And when you come back, just come in. You don't need to ask permission."

"Sure, I just feel weird walking into someone's house."

It was good to know that her foster parents had raised her to be polite. "It's not someone's house; it's your school, and somewhere I hope you will feel welcome."

"Oh, um... well, I do feel welcome, thanks. Anyway, is there something we can do while I'm here?"

"There's the history of the sidhe court," I said. I grinned when she groaned. "We can probably get you lighting candles with magic. But you will have to learn your history sometime."

"I am here, Quinn Larson." I heard the peep of Bud's voice calling from the front door.

"Who's that?" Dionne asked.

"Bud," Lionel answered. "She's going to learn how to be a leader from Quinn."

I got up and felt my way to the hall while Lionel explained to Dionne. "Are you alone, Bud?"

"Yes." She sounded impatient. "I am afraid of being seen, Quinn Larson. Please let me through the wards."

"You may come into the house at any time you are alone, or with your mother. Your access is restricted to the main floor unless accompanied by me or Lionel. You are bound by the apprentice oath."

I felt a rush of air past my face and then a tweak of my ear.

"Thank you, Quinn Larson. There were people coming. Human people! They are very frightening. How do you manage to live amongst them?"

Reaching up I held out my hand. "Please let go of my ear, Bud. Come and meet your fellow students."

She stepped onto my outstretched hand, giving my ear one more tweak as she did. "You said students. I thought you only had Lionel."

I walked her into the kitchen and felt her hop of excitement. "A girl! Is she the new witch? I heard about her!"

"This is Bud," I said in the direction I thought Dionne stood. "We are to teach her compassion and leadership. Bud, you know Lionel, and the young lady is Dionne, she is my new apprentice."

"You are so pretty, Dionne," Bud said as she flew off my hand.

"You're a fairy, cool," Dionne's voice was filled with awe.

There was no way we'd be able to pass her off as a visiting witch. Bud would have to know the whole story eventually. "Dionne is not familiar with all of our people. She is here for her own training as a witch."

I sat and reached for my mug as I listened to the two girls chatter. This was going to be interesting.

"I guess Princess dropped her off late," Lionel muttered next to me. "Should I go find out what happened?"

I took a sip of the, now cold, tea. "I think we can let it go until tomorrow. If she's late again, you can go talk to Princess while I do some teaching."

"I guess I can go study." He sounded so hopeful I didn't want to break it to him that I'd need his help with Bud. If I had the option of retreating into books, I might be tempted to, given the cheeky way Bud just took over.

"We need to work together today. I think Bud is getting too wound up to pay attention, so we can set some ground rules and send her home." I held up a hand hoping Bud and Dionne would notice. The chattering stopped, so I guess they were paying attention. "Dionne, I thought you needed to leave."

"Oh, I can stay for a while. Bud might need my help."

If I didn't know how anxious she was to learn her magic, I would suspect she'd been trying to get out of studying it today when she said her foster parents needed her. "Let us know when you need to go."

"Sure, can we do something other than the water boiling spell?"

I nodded. "Give me a minute to get organized. Bud, I want you to pay attention to Dionne's lesson. Then we'll focus on what you need to know."

"Yes, Quinn Larson, but I already know how to make water boil with magic." Her voice had calmed down to a level where it stayed in hearing range.

"You should listen to Quinn," Lionel said. "He is your teacher, so you shouldn't argue."

I started to tell Lionel to let me run the lessons, but Dionne cut me off.

"Lionel, don't be so mean. She wasn't arguing, she was just stating a fact."

"I wasn't being mean. She needs to know how things will work."

I held up my hand again, but this time the chatter continued.

"I pay attention to Quinn Larson. I took the oath, too." Bud's indignation was evident in the squeak of her voice.

Lionel sputtered, "I didn't mean you—"

"You are mean, Lionel," Bud squeaked.

"Lionel, you don't need to worry, we'll all get Quinn's time. Bud doesn't need the same lessons as I do, or you do," Dionne said.

"I know." Lionel's voice rose in desperation. "I just meant, with three of us, it was important that we behave."

"I am behaving and—." The rest of Bud's words were lost in a range I couldn't hear.

"Enough!" I slammed my hand on the counter. It hurt, but I knew better than to show it. Into the silence, I continued, "Lionel, I can deal with Bud. She is the heir to the Rose fairies, so I don't expect her to act like an apprentice."

"Yes, Quinn."

"Dionne, how long can you stay? Bud will need some of our time and I want you reading history as well as learning spells."

"I can stay an hour if I take the bus home."

"Good. Bud, why were you late?" Accountability was a leadership quality that even fairies needed to learn.

"My mother did not know whether you meant for me to start today. I convinced her that I should come."

At least she seemed anxious for the lessons. "When you go home, you can confirm with Princess that I meant every day."

"Yes, Quinn Larson."

Everyone seemed calmed down, so I continued to organize. "Lionel, please lead Dionne through a simple glamour spell. Have her disguise a bowl as a plate. You can do that down in the work room. Bud, you and I will talk for a while, then join them to see Dionne cast her spell before she goes home."

I waited but no one argued. "Okay, the last thing. I do not want to referee between you. I promise you all will have the training you need." *If it kills me.* "But please remember we have more on our hands than learning."

"Yes, Quinn," Lionel said. "Dionne, come on, I'm sure you'll get the hang of it quickly."

I heard them walk down the stairs, Lionel's voice explaining the steps Dionne would need to follow. "Bud, where are you?"

"I am here, Quinn Larson," she said, touching my hand.

"I guess the first thing we need to agree is how you don't get stepped on."

A trill of giggle rang in my ear. "I will be fine. My mother told me that it is my responsibility to make sure you know where I am. And I will not be this small for long. You know we grow fast."

I didn't see why her mother thought she needed training. Sure she was young, but she seemed to have a good heart. "Tell me what you think leading the Rose fairies entails."

4

Dionne had left as soon as she mastered the glamour spell. She learned fast, almost as fast as Lionel, when she wanted the knowledge. We were going to have to force some history on her if she kept going at the same rate. Magic without history was dangerous. Although I seem to remember history without magic was boring.

Bud was still with us, because she was afraid to go out until after dark. I told her she could run through the gardens without being noticed. It didn't help. Humans frightened Bud. That was healthy enough when you couldn't pass for human without a very strong glamour, but as a leader she couldn't let her fear rule her.

"You have many many books, Quinn Larson. Have you read them all?" Bud's voice came from the center of the workroom.

"No, I haven't. They are for research." I felt along the work-table for some paper so Lionel could make notes.

Bud touched my hand. "What have you been researching?"

I wondered if we'd left out any of the books. It wasn't like Lionel to be so careless, but it had been a weird day. "What does it look like to you? As a leader, you will need to draw your own conclusions, not ask for information to be spoon fed." Whether there were books out or not, she might be able to read the clues.

"Hmm, that is probably true, Quinn Larson." She leaned on my arm and I realized she had grown in the last two days. Fairies grew from a few inches at birth to their full height of about two feet in a few months. "Let me see what I think."

I waved Lionel over to my side. "Tell me what she is doing, quietly." If she was learning to work things out logically it would be a good step. If she was trying to take shortcuts, I had a long road ahead of me.

"She's poking at the earth where we had the circle," Lionel said. "Now she's tasting the dirt."

Deducting then, that was a good sign. It felt like she was trying, but it was not that long since she'd been babbling and bickering. I reminded myself to keep my expectations in check.

"You summoned a spirit. I don't know which one. Fairies don't talk to spirits."

Bud paused and I waited for Lionel to start the commentary again. But she started talking before he could. This time her voice came from the shelves behind me. "These books have been read recently. Quinn Larson, you should have Lionel clean more often."

Lionel stiffened. "I am not the maid, Bud. It is usually the newest apprentice who takes care of the house." Interesting new rule, since Lionel was my only apprentice up until a couple of weeks ago.

"I am not an apprentice," Bud snapped, destroying any hope I had that she'd gained some maturity.

"Stop arguing," I shouted. "Bud, besides the fact that we need to dust, what else have you learned?"

"I see that these books are about prophecy and omens. I think you have been researching a prophecy. An old one if you have to do all of this." She tapped me on the shoulder. "Did I pass?"

I couldn't help but chuckle. She was, indeed, trying. "You did well. Now, let's go upstairs and talk about how a good leader deals with conflict."

"Do I get to guess which prophecy?"

I stopped in mid-rise. Something about her words was too confident. "Bud, what would make you think you could guess?"

"I am a good guesser. I think you are looking for the prophecy of the six."

Lionel jerked beside me, and I couldn't bring myself to stop him from reacting. If Bud could guess so easily, we would have problems hiding Dionne's identity from anyone.

Before I could speak, Lionel asked, "Why do you think that?"

"Because there are rumors that three of the six have been found. Is it true? Is it a fairy? I know that one will be a fairy."

I tried not to breathe out my relief that she didn't know about Dionne. When we told her that Dionne was one of the six, the oath would keep our secret, but Dionne should be there for it. "I think the prophecy is about witches and wizards. Why do you think a fairy will be one of the six?"

"Because that is our lore. One of the six from the fairies, one from the forest, two from the wizards, two from the witches. When they come together, change will happen."

More than we knew this morning at least. "You guessed well, Bud. Now let's go and talk about conflict."

"I guessed right? Why did you want to research the prophecy? Do you know one of the six? This is very exciting."

I heard Lionel's groan. I nudged him and hoped he would understand that we would talk later.

"Bud, that's enough excitement for today. We have time to do your lesson before you leave. Let's have tea and honey. Tomorrow, perhaps, we'll talk more about the prophecy. But leadership is about more than just the exciting things."

"Yes, Quinn Larson." She was obviously trying to control her excitement, but it broke through in the giggle that punctuated her words.

When we were settled in the kitchen, Lionel and I with tea, and Bud with a saucer of honey, I started the lesson.

"A leader will often be faced with two sides of an argument and neither of them will be clearly right or wrong. Your job is to find a fair and just balance."

A slurp answered me, and then Bud said, "I would just decide. If one person was my friend, they would be right."

"Let's see how that will work. You and Lionel had a disagreement earlier. The problem is that my workroom is in need of more regular cleaning. Lionel is right that he is not the maid. You are right that you are not an apprentice. The room still requires cleaning, and I am not able to do that. How do we solve this?"

"I think Lionel should just clean. It's not fair to you to have a dirty workroom. Dionne cannot be here enough to spend time cleaning, and Lionel can take a bit of time out of his day to do it." She slurped some more honey as if the question was settled.

Lionel huffed, and I held out a hand to stop him. This was Bud's lesson. "But Lionel has his own studies. Your logic is good, but the outcome is not fair."

"Hmm. Well I am not going to do it. I'm too little. It would take too long."

"Fair enough. Can you think of a solution that allows Lionel to keep up his studies?" I was not going to give her the answer. If she couldn't figure it out, she would have it as homework tonight.

"If he made a spell to clean it then he would not have to keep doing it. Or is there a spell for cleaning?"

I remembered the hurricane he'd summoned in Cate's home and shook my head. The thought of Cate didn't hurt as much as it used to. I don't know if that was good, but at least it was progress. "No, that wouldn't be a good idea. If it got out of control, it would be a disaster."

"So, the room must be cleaned one time, and then a spell to stop the dust coming in. Then the only cleaning that needs to be done is after you do spells." She took a breath after her pronouncement.

I turned to where I hoped Lionel stood. "What do you think?"

"I could get the place cleaned pretty quickly. And if there isn't already a spell to keep the dust out, maybe I can create one." His excitement warmed his voice.

He was close to the point where I would let him create his own spell and graduate. I resigned myself to that happening sooner than I wanted. His studies were almost done.

"Sorry, Lionel, there is one. I should have thought of it sooner. Now, is it dark yet?"

"Yes. I should return to my mother. I hope she is feeling better. Goodnight, Quinn Larson and Lionel."

She pecked my cheek. I heard Lionel stomp down the hall. The door slammed a moment later, and Lionel came back.

"How long do you think her training will take?" he asked sounding fed up.

"It's not going to get easier, Lionel. I don't know how long it will take to train her up. I get the feeling that we don't know the whole story yet. I worry that Princess doesn't have long and won't see Bud become wise enough to lead the tribe."

He filled the kettle. "She learns fast. I think it will be okay. Princess will hang on long enough."

IT HAD BEEN A LONG DAY, AND I STILL HADN'T FIGURED OUT what I was going to do about Fionuir. The druids hadn't arrived by dinner time, but I was under no illusion they had forgotten about me.

"I think my decision isn't about releasing Fionuir," I said to Lionel over the barley soup he'd prepared. "It's all about the negotiations. If they think I accept too little, they will be asking us for help all the time."

"So, you will release her?" He sounded unsure. "I mean, she's not going to thank you for putting her there."

"I know, but I meant it when I said she's Maeve's problem. We'll need to talk to Maeve. If she is okay with it, then we'll do it as quickly as possible." I pushed away my empty bowl. "If the druids will agree to all of my conditions."

"And if they don't? Has anyone ever denied the druids what they want?"

"There's always a first time." I didn't want to be the one to test it, despite my words. "While we're waiting, what did you think of Bud's information about the prophecy?"

"I don't know. It does make sense that the six wouldn't just be wizards and witches. But fairies? They aren't the most stable of beings."

"That might be the point. If this is about change, stability won't be high on the list of attributes."

"Hm, maybe," he said. "We might be able to get more information from Moss, if there is one for the forest. Maybe we've been looking in the wrong place for information."

Moss wasn't a bad idea. If anyone knew about prophecy, it would be the guardian of the forest. Moss had lived in Stanley Park for as long as anyone could remember. If he'd ever come out in the past, I hadn't heard about it. Now, at about fifteen feet tall, he had to stay in there because no one had the power to cast, and maintain, a glamour strong enough to disguise him.

"Let's ask Beacon to approach him," I said. "Then we won't owe him a favor unless he has information."

No one wanted to owe Moss a favor, and no one could explain why. The sprite was wise, and helpful, and full of advice. Maybe his size was intimidating enough to imply he would expect something you didn't want to give. I shrugged aside the thought. "Eventually Beacon will start calling in favors. But I think asking him is a good idea. We can head into Banks' later."

The doorbell rang, and Lionel went to answer it. I hoped for druids, but you never know.

"The druids are back," Lionel announced.

I was going to have to find a way to teach him some perspective. He was in too much awe of them.

"We have come for your answer, Quinn Larson." The hollow voice came from in front of me.

I was tired of this anonymous approach. Knowing it was risky, I asked, "How many of you have come? And what are your names?"

For a moment, all I could hear was the tiny sounds of Lionel's fidgeting. Then, "I am Adair, to my right is Myrddin and to my left is Cenwyn. What is your decision?"

"Have you spoken to the council?"

"We have," the voice came from my left, so that was Myrddin. Now that I had a name, I could tell that the voice was not quite the same, a little lighter, maybe younger.

It didn't matter that I knew their names. I wasn't going to give ground. This was my home, and they were the ones wanting a favor. I was going to make it as difficult as I could without being outright rude. "And what was their answer to my conditions?"

"We have all agreed that Maeve must approve. You will ask her today. The council wishes to have this dealt with immediately." I couldn't tell which of the other two druids was speaking. So much for my improved perception of druid individuality.

"I will make arrangements as soon as possible. And what about Lionel's training?"

"It will be extended for one more month. We would expect it to start within a month of Fionuir's release," Myrddin said.

"That is not acceptable. I will manage the timing of Lionel's studies." And I wasn't ready to lose him until Dionne was settled into her training, or Bud graduated from leadership training.

There was a whispered conversation again. "We can extend the deadline for a year."

"Until I am ready. A year may still be too short."

"Very well, Quinn Larson. We will not negotiate on these petty matters any longer." It seems I hit a nerve. "And you will have your information if it is within our knowledge. Now, what is your decision?"

I pretended I had a choice in the matter. "If Maeve has no objections, and she can contain Fionuir, I will release her."

A skirl of whispers greeted my announcement. Then Adair, or possibly Cenwyn spoke. "The negotiation is not open. Fionuir's containment after her release is not our concern. If you release her from the prison you placed her in, then the souls will settle again. What she does afterward is not within the scope of our agreement. You need to release her as soon as Maeve gives you permission. And you will ensure that she gives you permission, wizard."

Druids were known for their lack of emotion, so it was surprising to sense anger in the words, and even more so to hear fear.

I wasn't going to back down. No one needed a vengeful sidhe running around, and that included the humans. Fionuir had gone on a killing rage before I contained her. In fact, that was the real reason I had to do it. Before I'd sent her into the dimensional fold, she'd been slaughtering humans to keep her place as Queen in the election. We'd managed to cover up the murders, but it could have revealed us to the humans. Something we would prob-ably not have survived.

"It is a concern for everyone," I said. "If she cannot be contained, then Fionuir will need to be imprisoned elsewhere. I will still release her from the dimensional fold, but I will need to find a different solution."

"This will cause a delay," Myrddin said. "That is not acceptable."

My temper was starting to fray. "I don't care. If you want to minimize the delay, I suggest you think of a new prison. She will not confine her rage to me. You let her take the amulet before, who's to say she won't take it again." The words were out before I could think of a way to soften them.

"Is this the information you wish us to provide? A new place to imprison your enemies?"

Damn druids, even in a crisis they tried to wiggle out of a deal by trickery. I wasn't going to jump in and let them give me information I didn't need or want. "No. This is information you will provide for free if you wish Fionuir released." I heard Lionel gasp. We would see what the druids made of my demand. I knew I had leverage, but how far could I push it?

"We will conduct research on a new prison. We will not provide you with this information unless necessary. We do not wish to provide you with a way to dispose of your enemies without cause."

I hoped I had no enemies, but I knew that was probably not the case. In fact, the hope died as I thought of the three other sidhe who hated me because I'd foiled their plan to release Fionuir. "Understandable. How do I contact you to let you know what Maeve decides?"

I heard the rustle of robes I took to mean they were getting ready to leave. "When you wish to communicate with the druids, you may do so through Myrddin."

I took it as a good sign that they'd thought through a communication channel. "And how to I get in touch with Myrddin?"

"Reach out your hand, wizard."

I did so, with some trepidation. Druids used all kinds of natural things for spell craft. I could as easily be in receipt of a magic snake as a twig spell. A few small papers hit my palm.

"When you wish to speak with Myrddin, burn one of the notes and he will attend you within twenty minutes."

I closed my hand around the paper and nodded. "Lionel, please show our guests to the door."

"Quinn," Lionel's voice preceded him into the room when he

returned. "I'm not sure you should have been so rude. They might decide to... I don't know. Punish you in some way."

"I wasn't rude, Lionel. I was firm." I could sense his real worry like a chill in the room. "They won't do anything to me, at least until they get Fionuir freed."

"And then? They have some old magic. You might find yourself bound to a lake or trapped in your house."

"Lionel, don't worry. They will honor the training time. They might make you work for any real information, but they will train you."

"That's not what I was worried about. I guess I'm worried that they'll find a way to stop you training Dionne. If we can't train her, what will happen to her?"

A good question. "If something happens to me, the best thing you can do is to talk to Moss. He'll know a way to find another wizard to train her; a wizard or maybe a witch. And he'll make sure you can graduate."

And I'd have to figure out a plan B. The druids were the least of my worries. If Maeve didn't keep Fionuir under control, there might be sidhe after my life, too.

5

W e were having breakfast the next day waiting for Bud to arrive and discussing how to set up her leadership training, when the doorbell rang.

"Why would Bud ring the bell?" Lionel asked.

"She wouldn't. Maybe it's the druids." I hoped not. I needed some space between visits. And some time to get Maeve on side with the plan.

I heard him talking to a woman. I couldn't make out the words, and her voice wasn't familiar. Footsteps came down the hall. "Come in. Quinn is in the kitchen. You are welcome there."

That was a weird way to set the wards, like he was hiding the fact that he was setting them. Who could he be inviting just to the kitchen?

"Quinn, this is Louise Metcalfe. She's a social worker and wants to talk to you about Dionne."

Social worker? Human. I would have preferred an entire academy of druids.

Lionel coughed. "Maybe I should go do some more studying? In my room?"

And leave me alone with a human, a government employee at

that? "No. Why don't you put the kettle on? Ms. Metcalfe, would you like some tea?"

"I don't have a lot of time today, Mr. Larson. We will need to set an appointment soon to review Dionne's work environment. But today we'll just have a chat, so I can be sure this job is good for her."

I pointed toward the couch. "Why don't we get more comfortable? Please, join me in the living room." This clearing the wards was much harder when you couldn't let the person know you were doing it. There was no way I could let her have any access to the house without me present. I took the couch and gestured to the chair I knew was across from me.

"Fine," she said. "I have a few questions. I understand you are sight disabled?"

"Yes. I'm blind, although there is hope that the condition will reverse itself." I couldn't give up the belief that I'd find the spell to reverse what Fionuir had done to me. "Lionel lives here and helps me where I need it."

"It's not a problem. We don't discriminate based on disability. Now, Dionne will be working here after school, is that correct?"

"Yes. And weekends when necessary." I heard the kettle boil and hoped Lionel would join us rather than slink off to his room. I kind of liked humans, but they scared me up close. If I was going to have to talk to this woman on a regular basis, I'd need some advice from Olan. As a pixie, he couldn't be present, but as someone charged with protecting humans, maybe he had some insights to make me feel more comfortable.

"That is acceptable as long as she has time to socialize."

"Tea," Lionel said. I felt him sit beside me on the couch.

Ms. Metcalfe thanked him but didn't pause to sip. "What work will she be doing for you?"

I remembered Dionne saying office work. "We'll be setting up a new business. Dionne will be helping us get things organized and setting up our systems."

"Can I see her work area?"

"It's a mess right now. We'll make sure it's ready for your next visit." Dionne was going to have to work on creating our 'office' when she arrived.

"What kind of business?"

Another thing we'd have to work out. It was starting look like Dionne's magical training was going on hold until we came up with a cover story that would pass inspection. "I would prefer not to discuss that right now. I don't want any competitors finding out what we're doing. Would you sign a non-disclosure agreement?"

I heard paper rustling. "No. I'm afraid we don't do that. However, if you are willing to sign this document to say your business is not illegal or immoral, we can put it aside for now. I'll examine the space for safety, and you'll have three months to provide us with a brief on your activity."

Paper touched my hand, and I passed it to Lionel. "What does it say?"

He took the document and read it out loud. He finished by saying, "So, it's just what she said. You are promising you are not exposing Dionne to anything illegal or immoral."

"What exactly do you mean by immoral?" I didn't want to sign any document with such a vague statement. It might be different for humans, but if I put my signature on the document, it had the force of an oath.

"Prostitution, drugs, fraud, adult entertainment," Ms. Metcalfe recited.

"Aren't those things illegal?"

"Well, adult entertainment isn't, but we don't want our children involved. Yes. The other things are illegal."

I couldn't tell if she was getting annoyed or was just tired of dealing with me. She didn't sigh, but there was no emotion in her voice.

"I'm not willing to sign a document that isn't clear. I don't want someone determining the validity of what we are doing by some moral code. Can we remove the morality statement?" I was so tempted to send a confidence spell her way to make her feel no need to ask for anything, but it was too risky because she might report to someone who wouldn't take her word for how innocent this deal was. And I couldn't very well tell Dionne she couldn't cast spells to get what she wanted when I did it.

"If you can't tell me what your business is, I have to be cautious." Definitely annoyed this time, I was making her job hard, and we must be the first call in a long Monday of visits.

"Okay, that's fair. I wouldn't want Dionne exposed to a shady business either. I'll sign it, but I want it revoked when you have assessed the business." Well the business that we mockup, and it will be moral if it kills me.

"Do you need a pen?"

I held out my hand, not wanting to waste time while Lionel searched for one. As I signed where Lionel placed the pen, I whispered a charm into the ink that would fade it to invisibility over the next month. It wouldn't break my obligation, but it would keep me out of the human court system.

"Thank you," Ms. Metcalfe said when I handed the paper to her. "Now we need to set a time for me to inspect the work arrangements. It would be best to do this when Dionne is here."

It was time to be accommodating. "We will sort out the workspace in the next day or so. We can't make any progress until we do anyway."

I heard papers flipping. "I have time tomorrow around four pm. Will that work?"

"I'll make it work. Will you be able to sign off on Dionne's job tomorrow?" Maybe that would be the last visit we had to endure.

"Possibly. I need assurance that she will have an appropriate pay level, but we should be able to get out of your hair quickly. Now I must leave. I have another appointment. I'll see you tomorrow."

While Lionel let her out, I revoked any permissions that

might have been set while she was here. At least we'd managed unscathed this time. I am not sure that would continue.

"How are we going to get a workspace ready by tomorrow?" Lionel asked.

"Part real, part glamour. We have today to clean out part of the attic, and Dionne will have to come up with the answers to all the questions."

BUD DIDN'T ARRIVE ON TIME, SO I HAD TO SPARE LIONEL TO GO find her.

"How are you going to deal with the attic?"

"I can feel around up there and figure out what the size of the problem is." I tried to sound hopeful, but he was right, I could only get so much done alone, and we didn't have all day.

"Maybe we should just let Bud come when she's ready?"

This was just wasting time. "Why? Don't you want to go?"

"I don't want to leave you here alone. That woman may come back, or the druids."

Ah, what he meant was that he didn't want to miss a visit by the druids. Unfortunately, we didn't have time for this. Princess wasn't going to last much longer, and Bud needed training. "Go find Bud. Be back as soon as you can, and let Princess know that she needs to get Bud here every morning. If there's a problem, Bud can hide in the shrubs until we call her, but I'm not chasing after her."

"Do you want me to tell her in that tone of voice?" Lionel asked. "Or was that just for my benefit?"

Where had he learned that attitude? Probably Dionne. I would have told him to be more respectful if he didn't have a point. My annoyance was better aimed at Dionne, or Bud. "Sorry. I'll leave it to you to decide what tone of voice to use with Princess. I'll be upstairs trying to figure out what to do with everything there while you're gone."

He promised to be less than an hour and then the door banged shut.

I felt my way upstairs and paused at the door to the attic. Well, it was not a real attic, it was a finished room, but the walls were bare, and I'd always used it as a storage locker. I pushed open the door trying to visualize how it had looked last time I was able to see it. I remembered random stacks of boxes that I'd simply put wherever I could find a space.

I shuffled through the doorway with my hands held out to stop my fall if I tripped. It might just be a case of organizing the boxes and pretending the desks and equipment were on order. Pushing the mess into shape might help my temper, which was not settling as I hoped. If Dionne hadn't told her foster parents she was working for me, we wouldn't have social workers inspecting my home. I had enough on my plate with the druids, a potentially homicidal sidhe royalty to free, and a fairy princess to train.

Making sense of the room was difficult because everywhere I touched, there was a box, or two boxes piled. I'd lost track of where I stood in the room, and I wasn't sure any more how long I'd been in there. There was too much mess for me to find a wall to follow. Rather than stumble around increasing my frustration, I pressed on the nearby boxes to find one firm enough for a seat. Lionel would be back soon and it wouldn't hurt me to do some quiet thinking.

I created a mental list of my priorities. First, we needed to set up this workspace and it would have to be the minimal amount of effort. Then I needed to go see Maeve. Then I needed to figure out how to pay Dionne for her work. Then... by the time I got the first two things done, I'd be facing Ms. Metcalfe without a plan.

I decided to clear my mind and worry about fixing everything when Lionel came back. He was less an apprentice now than a peer with less experience. Maybe he could take something off me.

And maybe I should start planning his transition from apprentice to full wizard. And maybe I should stop adding items to my list.

"Quinn?" Lionel's voice woke me from a light doze.

"Up here." At least now I had someone to lead me out of the maze.

I heard him climb the stairs, two of them creaking as he put his weight on them. "Wow, this will be a great place to work. Maybe we should set up a library when the social services thing is over."

"I'm worried that will never be over. Or at least for the next couple of years. When Dionne turns eighteen, she won't be their kid any longer."

"Does that mean she won't be living with her foster parents?"

"I don't know. Let's not add that to our problems just now. Is Bud here?"

"No. She'll be here later. There was a tribe meeting going on. Apparently, there is some problem with Bud taking over the leadership."

Normally the current leader chose the heir. If there were concerns, it meant that Bud had done something to make the tribe worried. "We'll have to find out what Bud has done to make it questionable whether she can be the queen. Princess should have told us. Then again why did I expect her to be totally up front with us?"

"I'm sure it's not that bad. Fairies can get upset about the silliest things." He touched my arm. "Bud will be here in a few hours. Do you want me to get you out of here?"

I shook my head. "We need to deal with this. Just tell me what to do to help."

LIONEL AND I HAD THE UPSTAIRS ORGANIZED BY THE TIME Dionne arrived with Bud running behind her. Lionel had cast the spell to keep dust away over the whole house, now everything just needed cleaning.

I had everyone in the kitchen for a talk. "Bud and Dionne, you'll do the cleaning today."

"Why us?" Dionne said. "Why can't Lionel help?"

I held up my hand. "I'm getting to that. Dionne, we had a visit from a social worker today."

"Yeah, they were bound to come and check you out. What happened?"

Suppressing my desire to yell at her for the cavalier attitude, I told her what had happened. "And we have our inspection tomorrow."

"It sounds like it went well. I can help get us ready for the visit. I've been thinking that the business could be a job site, or a retailer. I'll find something tomorrow on the computers at school. I have last period free, so I can get here before she does."

The optimism of the young failed to inspire me. "It's not that simple, but I'm sure we can survive it and then get on with our business. Before we agree on anything about the job, Dionne, I have to have your word that you won't put us in this position again. If we are exposed as wizards and witches to the humans, it could mean death to us and possibly all of our friends."

"I'm human." She sounded shocked that I suggested she wasn't.

I tried to be gentle with her. "No, you were raised by humans, and you look human, but you are Real Folk. You've heard of the witch trials?" Her quiet yes let me continue. "Then you know what can happen."

"Don't be so mean, Quinn Larson," Bud said. "She didn't know the human would be trouble."

I turned in what I hoped was her direction, a stern look on my face. "I am not finished, Bud. I have things to ask you as well."

"Oh," her voice squeaked. It made me wonder what she thought I was going to ask.

I turned back to Dionne. "Can you promise not to bring any other authorities here? To keep us safe from discovery?"

"No," she said.

That wasn't what I expected. I couldn't refuse to teach her, but I needed her cooperation.

"Look, I've learned a bit about making promises," she rushed to say before I could speak. "I promise to not bring any other authorities on purpose, but I don't know who might want to get involved. It's not that long until I age out of the system. I think I can keep us safe, but I can't promise. I'm not in control of that."

I was proud of her for thinking it through, but frustrated that we might – no make that probably would – have to deal with humans again before she was eighteen. At least the apprentice oath would help to keep her from making mistakes. "That will have to be good enough." I turned in Bud's direction. "Now, Bud."

"Yes, Quinn Larson." Her voice was barely in the audible range.

"Why do the Rose fairies want someone else to lead them?"

"Who told you that?"

"I did," Lionel said. "The tribe meeting today was to talk about you as a suitable leader."

"They decided to give me a chance. It is because you are training me, Quinn Larson." The little wheedle in her voice was meant to soften me.

I tried not to let it work. "That's not what I asked. It is good to know that they trust me, but I need to know why they don't want you."

"I don't want to tell you." Bud rubbed my cheek with hers. "It was a long time ago. Let's get to that cleaning."

Bud was maybe four months old. "I still need to know."

She burst into tears, and there was nothing but sobs for so long I started to wonder if we needed to cast a calming spell on her. She finally blew her nose and started talking. "I made a big mistake. I took other babies with me on an adventure." She was hiccupping now from crying. "One baby didn't look when we danced near the fire. She fell in."

The grief and regret flowed from her like a wave. "She was my friend. Her name was Apricot Nectar. She was funny, and she loved me. And she died. And I miss her. And I'm so sorry about it."

I fished for a tissue, knowing it would be far too big for her, but needing to do something. The council was right that Bud would be a poor leader without training. They were wrong about the kind of training.

"Thank you for telling us," I said passing the tissue. "I am sorry about your friend."

She blew her nose before saying, "Will you still train me?"

"Yes."

A deep sigh escaped before she spoke again, "Can I ask a question, Quinn Larson?"

If I didn't know fairies well, I would be suspicious of how quickly she got over the tears. "You can always ask questions, that is how you learn."

"What is a social worker?"

I wasn't sure I knew how to answer that without confusing her and talking in circles. "Dionne, can you explain?"

"Sure. They are people who look after my safety and education until I'm ready to take care of myself."

"Oh, I understand. Quinn Larson, you are my social worker. Okay, Dionne, let's go clean and then we can do more interesting things."

6

Bud and Dionne had the office clean in a half hour. They didn't complain or argue. They just went up and cleaned it.

"Do you have a table or something?" Dionne asked as she clumped down the stairs. "We could set up a little coffee section."

"No. I don't think that's necessary. We need to keep this simple. When Ms. Metcalfe arrives, we'll tell her that the desks and computers are on order. You will come tomorrow with a couple of choices on business model." I was doing my best to convince everyone that things would go well in the faint hope that it would convince me. "When the social worker is here, Bud, you need to be quiet, and you need to stay downstairs."

"Couldn't I just go home, Quinn Larson?"

"No, we'll still have time to do lessons after she's gone."

"But I am scared of humans."

Lionel clicked his tongue in annoyance. "Bud, you need to be brave if you are going to be a leader."

"Lionel, that's enough." He was right, but his tone was going to cause an argument soon. "Bud, you'll be safe, the human will not be able to go down to the workroom."

"Okay," she said, reluctance dripping from the word.

I would have to talk to Lionel later about cultivating a little patience with Bud, because he might have to work with her as the leader of the Rose fairies. But that would be later when we were alone, now we needed to get ready for a visit to the sidhe court. "Lionel, can you go down to the workroom and summon Melbe. Ask him to arrange for us to speak to Maeve today, if possible."

"Sure." He sounded brighter, probably because I trusted him to do something delicate. "When do you want to meet her?"

"Within the hour. I'll get Dionne prepped and then we'll change for court." I realized I was only thinking about how I looked. Dionne might be totally inappropriately dressed. Bud, didn't need to worry because the sidhe would pretend she wasn't there. They were related, but neither fairy nor sidhe would admit it.

It might be a bad idea to just ask what a woman was wearing, but I counted on the fact that she'd forgive a blind wizard. "Dionne, what are you wearing?" If it wasn't appropriate for court, we'd have to do something with my meager selection of beads and scarves.

"Nothing special. A white shirt with a black cardigan, and a skirt."

That didn't help. "Bud, is she dressed well enough for court?"

"Hmm, I think if she had some sparkly things added, she would be fine. Do you have any sparkly things, Quinn Larson?"

As a matter of fact, since jewelry was good for hiding charms, I did. "Look in the box on my dressing table." I said the words to give her access to my room. "While she's getting your jewels, we need to talk about the sidhe."

"Have I seen any sidhe? Oh, that's so pretty. Are you sure I can wear it?"

I didn't care what it looked like. I trusted Bud, and anyway Lionel would tell me if it wasn't appropriate. "No, there weren't any at Banks'. We'll be going to the court and there are some rules. And there are a few problems."

"What rules? Are they complicated?"

"No. I mean, yes. The rules of the court are very complicated, but you'll just need to do two things. First don't speak unless you have to."

"How will I know I have to?"

Part of me wanted her to stay safely in my house, but my job was to train her. And since we were going to free one of them, she'd have to meet the sidhe sometime. "If Maeve asks you a question you will need to answer. Don't volunteer anything, only answer her question, and be respectful. That's the second rule."

"Okay, but if this Maeve is so scary, why do you need to talk to her. Isn't there someone who likes you?"

"Maeve does like me." I hoped that was still true. "The sidhe are complicated."

"Okay," Dionne said. "I get it. I'll be good."

Bud giggled.

"No, that's enough," Dionne said with a laugh. "I can only wear one set of earrings and two necklaces is plenty."

"Lionel will disguise us for the walk. If Bud wants you to wear more jewelry, you probably should. Just make sure I get it back before you go home. I don't want the social worker to come here looking for an explanation about why I'm giving you such special gifts."

"Only one more bracelet, and you are perfect." Bud's pleasure at the task was evident in every word.

"Bud, I want you to promise you won't take offense at anything that happens in the court."

She wrapped her arms around my neck. "I can come?"

"Yes. If you can behave." Every nerve was telling me to leave her at home. But given what she'd just told me about her history, she needed to learn how to balance her excitement with sense. "Do you promise?"

"Yes. I will be polite, and quiet, and smile, and whatever you wish. I have never been to court, no one I know has been there. I hear it is beautiful."

Lionel clomped up the stairs before I could say anything. "We have an audience in half an hour. You look great, Dionne. Let's get changed, Quinn. I'll put your suit out."

WE STOOD ACROSS FROM THE WAREHOUSE THAT HELD THE SIDHE court. I waited for Lionel to tell us when it was safe to go. I had worked out a way to fend for myself at home, but when I was outside, it was hard to hear my way around with all the people and traffic.

"There are two new guards," Lionel said. "Not twins."

"You mean those two homeless guys?" Dionne was whispering. "Is that the court?"

"Yes. I think we need to train your real sight. You should see two sidhe men dressed in deep blue court dress holding ebony lances tipped in silver," Lionel said. "Bud, settle down. The spell won't contain you if you keep hopping around."

The longer we stood here, the more likely something would go wrong. "Let's leave the lesson until later. Can we cross now?"

"Yes," Dionne said. "Let's go. I want to see this court. Will I need this real sight?"

I felt her tug my arm and stepped forward. "No. When we get inside the glamours will drop, all the glamours. So, Bud, you'll be visible. Remember to behave yourself."

"I will, Quinn Larson."

We came to a stop and I heard a shuffle of cloth that must have been the guards coming to attention. "Quinn Larson and friends to see Queen Maeve." I waited for the attitude I was used to from the twins.

"She is waiting for you." A warm tenor voice responded. "The door is open inside."

A refreshing change. I hoped that it would stay friendly. I was tired of having to fight my way into, or out of, the court.

The sound of the street faded completely a few steps into the hall. The court was in the center of an old warehouse.

Dionne was going to be amazed. The scent of lemon incense preceded the clink of glasses and the chatter as we approached the door.

"Oh, it's beautiful," Dionne breathed. "Quinn, it's like a picture book."

I remembered exactly what it looked like when Fionuir was queen. It had been lovely, if you didn't know about the poisonous undertow of the court intrigues. Now Maeve was queen, it was less vile, but the politics were uncertain. "Remember, don't speak unless spoken to. If they knew what you were, you might not survive the day."

"What?" Bud whispered from my shoulder. "Don't you mean who she is?"

"We will talk about it another time." I couldn't sense Lionel. I thought he'd entered a few steps in front of me. "Lionel?"

"He's talking to some guy," Dionne said. "Are all the sidhe so pretty?"

"Yes, it's part of being a sidhe. Can you describe the man?" I hoped it wasn't Owen or Garnet, but it wouldn't be so quiet if it was.

Dionne sighed. "He's dressed in lavender silk and cream lace. He looks like a sidhe, I guess. Red hair. Lionel's coming back."

"Maeve will be ready for us soon," Lionel said. "There are some chairs in the corner." He guided me by my elbow. I kept my other hand on Dionne's arm, so she had no choice but to come with us.

"Don't accept any food," I said as we sat in well-upholstered chairs.

"Why, is it magic?" Her voice vibrated with excitement.

"No, but you don't know which dishes are free of alcohol, and I don't want to send you home drunk."

Dionne giggled. "Ms. Metcalfe wouldn't be happy about that."

A waft of cinnamon heralded the first of the sidhe. I knew we would need to deal with curiosity, but I was hoping Dionne would have a few minutes to enjoy the scene before she got interrogated.

"Quinn Larson, do you know me?" The voice was female and musical, but not familiar.

"I apologize if I have forgotten, but it is difficult to recognize someone by just their voice. No matter how lovely it is." I crossed my fingers that no one was rolling their eyes at my words.

"I am Niav. We have met only once, but I believe you were intoxicated at the time. Now, to apologize properly for your behavior, introduce me to your lovely companion."

"I'm his new apprentice."

"Oh, how wonderful." Niav was almost giggling with the idea that she was learning about someone new.

"Apprentice, I will speak for you." Before I could add anything, I heard the rustle of another sidhe's clothes. "Quinn, don't be such a spoil sport. Introduce us. It is so seldom we get to meet someone new." That voice I did know. It was Ailin. I hadn't expected him to be allowed in the court. His punishment for leading an unsuccessful rebellion seemed far too short to me. "Dionne is new to the city. She arrived a few days ago." I introduced the two sidhe, and when she didn't say anything, I was relieved to know Dionne remembered the rules.

"We must find time to talk," Niav said. "Perhaps while Quinn is speaking to Maeve?"

"Dionne will need to be with me when I speak to the Queen."

"A pity," Ailin answered. "No matter. We will find a time to talk soon."

Great, now I was going to have to make sure Dionne wasn't left alone to be interrogated by anyone. Lionel would have to escort her home every day unless I could make her off limits. Perhaps Maeve would help.

"Don't fret about Ailin," Niav said with a sniff. "He is under house arrest along with his co-conspirators. Your little friend will be safe for a few more months, I think. Maeve was very annoyed."

"Thank you, Niav. That's good to know. I fear her training will be interrupted if she spends too much time with him."

"You are brave bringing a fairy here. I hope you have her on an appropriate leash. It would be a great pity if she offended anyone."

I could feel Bud's wings vibrating in offense, but she stayed quiet and beside me. "I am also training her. I don't expect to be here long enough to offend any but the most sensitive."

"Let us hope that only the thick skinned are here tonight. I see Maeve is ready. Allow me to escort you." Her hand touched mine, and I rose.

"Lionel, Dionne, please bring Bud and follow us." I took Niav's elbow and let her lead me to Maeve. I could feel the gaze of the court follow us across the room and started to wonder if I would have to fight my way out of the court again.

"Bring chairs for my guests," Maeve's voice rose over the chatter. "Three chairs. I assume the fairy will stand beside yours, Quinn. So you can control her."

Nice way to say I will keep her under control or else. "Of course. How are you, Maeve?" A tap on my shoulder preceded the touch of the chair behind my knee. I sat.

"The court does well, so I am well. We are preparing for a feast so I cannot dally. What business do you have with me?"

No invitation to join the feast. I was relieved because I would have had to decline but insulted for Bud. I was pretty sure Maeve had excluded us because of her. Okay, if she was going to blunt, then I'd take it as a cue. "We need to release Fionuir, and I am hoping you can contain her."

Maeve laughed, a warm and stirring sound. "Oh, is that all.

Such a trivial request. Well, I am flattered that you believe you need my permission to release her. She is my subject, but she is your prisoner. I can contain her if necessary. I would prefer if you left her where she is for a little longer."

Pretty words, but I'm sure she would have felt differently if I hadn't asked permission. "It seems her imprisonment is causing difficulties."

"For whom?"

Now that was a problem. Maeve wouldn't care about the druids' concerns. In fact, if they had been more diligent about keeping the Gur amulet secure, Fionuir wouldn't have been able to do the damage she had. The druids hadn't said to keep this a secret, but they hadn't said I could share it either. "I am not able to say. Does it matter? I thought you would prefer to have her in your control rather than leave me as the holder of the keys to her prison."

A teacup was placed in my hand. I thanked whoever had served me. I heard Lionel caution Dionne and relaxed a little. He would take care of both the girls. I could concentrate on my conversation with Maeve. I couldn't let my guard down just because she seemed to be reasonable – there was always something hidden beneath a sidhe smile.

"I am happy with the situation. I trusted you to keep her in place."

I sipped the tea, some herbal concoction that refreshed despite the bitterness. "I hope you can continue to trust me when I say it is vital that I release her."

"Who is your young friend? It is unusual to meet a new witch."

I could give a bit of information without endangering Dionne. I just hoped I could keep it to just a bit. "She is visiting, and I am assessing her abilities."

"You have changed, Quinn Larson. I seem to remember you were determined to remain a solitary wizard. And now you have two apprentices and a... fairy." The last word came out as though she'd tasted something foul.

"We all grow, Maeve." The chatter of the court had been fading away as we talked. Now there was silence behind me. They were waiting for something. If it was information about Dionne, they would be disappointed. If it was to see how Maeve would handle me, well I was also waiting for that.

"I acknowledge that I owe you a boon for your help with my recent rebellion, such as it was, but I do not wish to release my rival without good reason. What if she should escape between your custody and mine?"

"I believe I can release her directly to you." It should work. I just didn't have any proof and no way to practice. "The dimensional fold exists in all points in this dimension at the same time."

"And why would I feel secure that she will appear where I wish her, rather than some remote mountaintop?"

"I am confident that will not happen. It is all in the spell."

There was a long pause. So long that the court started chatting again. Did they think this was over? I couldn't let it be. If I had to come back, then I would. The more Maeve resisted, the more I felt the compulsion to do as the druids asked. Was she casting a spell over me? Was she trying to send a message? If she was, it would not be for my benefit.

"Maeve, I think you and I have enough history that we should be able to trust a little. Fionuir caused me so much loss. Do you think I would release her for no reason? Do you think Cate's life meant so little? My eyesight?"

Still no response. I trusted that Lionel would tell me if she'd left. I put the teacup on my knee. "I won't keep you any longer, Maeve. As you said, you have a feast to attend. Perhaps we can talk again."

"Do not be so hasty, Quinn Larson. I am considering your request. You ask much of me without giving anything in return."

I relaxed. She was looking for a way to say yes. I had one thing

I could give that was mine. "I will relinquish any claim of revenge on Fionuir. You may do with her as you please." Even Maeve couldn't deny me my revenge, but I wasn't interested in getting any.

It still hurt that Cate was taken from me just as we were becoming more than just friends. I was still blind, but I had come to value other things. Lionel had brought me back to life with his care and curiosity. Dionne... well Dionne had actually been responsible for Cate's death – but it had been a real mistake.

"That is generous of you. Very well, you may release her. I will need to know when you plan to do this so I can make the arrangements for her new prison."

I nodded and moved to put the teacup on the floor. It was taken from me before I managed to. "I will send Lionel with the information about timing. Thank you for your attention. Please enjoy the feast."

"Perhaps another time you can stay." The *when you do not have the fairy with you* was apparent.

I wondered how to make it up to Bud. I'd known the sidhe wouldn't like her being there, but not that they would be so insulting to her. A leader didn't generally have to deal with that kind of behavior. But then, as the leader of the Rose tribe she would have little or no contact with sidhe.

"I look forward to it, Maeve." I gestured to my companions and felt Lionel's hand on my arm to lead me out.

❧ 7 ❧

We made it out and across the street with no resistance. Maeve really did run a more civilized court than Fionuir.

"I'm sorry, Bud." I wanted to restore her good humor after the way she'd been treated in the court. She hadn't spoken for a while, and I figured she was fuming, perhaps because I would have been. "I should have left you out of this visit. I didn't know it would be that bad."

"I am glad you did not leave me at your house. I learned many things." She didn't sound upset. "I am the first fairy to go to the court in the memory of my tribe. This will help me to make amends for my foolishness. I have information that may be useful."

Bud was learning restraint. The flush of pride I felt was a surprise. "I commend you for not reacting to the insults. Please, do not attack the court until we are finished with Fionuir."

She patted my knee. "I know we need them for this venture, Quinn Larson. Besides, I think we can use information in other ways than fighting."

"We should get back," Lionel said. "I don't know how much longer Dionne will have before she needs to go home."

"I can stay later if it's important. Isn't Banks' near here? Could we go there for just a little visit?" She wrapped her arm around mine and leaned in a little. Her ability to overcome the fact I couldn't see was scary.

I wanted to say no, that she needed to start focusing on her magic training, but her voice was so pitiful. Despite knowing it was on purpose, and something that had worked for her in the past, I couldn't deny that part of her training was about other Real Folk. "We need to eat, I suppose. Remember what I told you last time?"

"No beer even if people offer it to me. Be careful what I tell people about myself. And don't stare." The words came out on a huff.

"It's important, Dionne." I was starting to get nervous that Lionel's glamour on Bud would fade before we got into a safe place. "Until you have some control over your power, it would be dangerous for someone to find out who you are."

Bud's voice piped up. "What do you mean, Quinn Larson? Why would Dionne be in danger?"

I shushed her. We would have to tell Bud what Dionne's secret was before she accidentally made people curious. "Later, Bud. Let's get into Banks' before humans start to wonder what's going on."

A pull on my jeans started me walking. "That I can agree on. There are too many humans here for me to be happy," Bud said.

The rumble of voices and aroma of roasting meat greeted us as we stepped through the door to Banks'. Bud squealed and then asked permission to join some friends. I agreed because it would be easier to talk if she was involved in something else.

"Beacon is here," Lionel said. "Shall we join him?"

That was lucky. These days, Beacon was usually deep in Stanley Park doing tasks for his grandfather, Moss. It wasn't official, but most people thought Beacon was being trained to take over from Moss when he returned to the earth. That meant Beacon would spend weeks at a time in the wild areas of Stanley Park, working with the imps and other sprites to keep the trees healthy. "Ask Mark to send a round over, tea for Dionne. Let's see if he has any information about the prophecy."

Lionel led us to the table and excused himself to get the drinks.

"Add a whiskey for Olan. He's on his way in a few minutes," Beacon said. "So, this is Dionne?"

"Yes. Dionne, this is Beacon." I kept it short because I wondered if Moss had told Beacon about her powers. It wasn't that I didn't trust Beacon, I just didn't want to tell him in the crush of Banks'. You never knew who might hear no matter how quiet you were.

My concern must have shown on my face because Beacon said, "Yes, he told me all about you, Dionne. How is your introduction to your powers going?"

Lionel placed our drinks down, pushing mine against my fingers, before Dionne answered.

"It's going slowly, but I love it. Should I come with you to visit Moss? He was so nice to me. I want to talk to him again."

I held up my hand. "Before we have any more trips to visit people, you need to study. I do have a favor to ask you, Beacon."

"You are always after favors, Quinn," Olan's voice cut in. "Thanks for the whiskey. What can we do for you?"

I owed Olan a lot. He'd helped me solve the human murders, which led to imprisoning Fionuir. In the process, he'd been turned into a chickadee by The Morrigan. It had been reversed, but I still felt I owed him my life. What I didn't owe him was Dionne's safety.

"I'm looking for some information. I've set Dionne and Lionel a research task. They need to find information on the prophecy of the six. I figured that would keep them busy for a while." *Shut up. Babbling will make him suspicious.*

"And this is Dionne?"

"Yes." I introduced them and used the cover story we'd made up. "Maybe you can drop by the house, Olan. Later tonight."

"I'm busy later tonight. I could come by tomorrow afternoon."

This was slipping out of control. I sipped at the beer and took a moment to choose my words, grateful that Dionne and Lionel were keeping silent. "Tomorrow afternoon isn't a good idea. We are working on a critical stage of Dionne's training. Tomorrow after dark?"

"I'll be there. Now, I think you have things to talk about that I am not to hear. I'll be off to gossip with my friends."

"Oh, please stay," Dionne said. "I would love to talk about pixies."

"Then come with me," Olan said. "I can introduce you to people. It's hard being new to town. I know because I travel a fair bit. What do you say, Quinn?"

My head told me I'd have to let her loose and then trust that she wouldn't talk about her powers. Unfortunately, the same head imagined all the repercussions of a slip on her part.

I felt a tug on my hand. "Please, Quinn. I remember what you said."

If I could see who was around, I wouldn't feel so worried – at least that's what I told myself.

"I'll keep an eye on her," Lionel said. "There are only a few sidhe here, and Olan won't give them the time of day. Bud will help too."

"Fine, just be careful," I said suppressing a shiver of fear.

Dionne kissed my cheek and left. I wondered if Olan might just send her back to get some peace. "Lionel, don't rely on Bud too much. She doesn't know what Dionne is."

"You have to tell her, Quinn," Lionel said. "We need to be able to talk frankly around her."

"I know. I'll do it soon, but let's not waste Beacon's time."

"Oh, no problem. I'm happy to be here as long as you need me to. If I go back to the park early, Moss will just find something more for me to do. Now, tell me why Bud is with you."

Mark refilled our drinks, and I told Beacon about Princess' problem. "I don't think it's a secret, but I'd prefer you didn't talk about it. Now, do you know anything about the prophecy?"

"I probably know what you do, more or less. We keep our eyes open for any sign that our part of the six has arrived, but as far as I know they haven't."

"It was news to us that the six weren't all wizards and witches," Lionel said. "What exactly do you know?"

I sat back and let him ask. It was the only way I would know if he had matured enough to graduate.

"Two wizards, two witches, a fairy folk and a forest folk. They will have all the powers and when they come together nothing will be the same."

"Any idea why it's not evenly split?" Lionel asked.

"No. But my guess is because other than the druids, you are the only Real Folk who search for knowledge outside your own species. Perhaps that will make a difference." I heard him plunk his glass on the table. "As much as I would prefer to stay, I think you are in a hurry for this information. I should go now and ask Moss what he knows."

When he'd gone, I swallowed the last of my beer and asked Lionel to gather our two missing students. I wondered how long it would be before he realized that we had a new piece of information. Bud had said fairy, Beacon fairy folk. My heart twisted at the thought of one of six being a sidhe.

BY THE TIME WE CORRALLED BUD AND DIONNE TO LEAVE, WE had to arrange for a taxi. It was rare for one of the Real Folk to need the services of a cab, but Dionne used her cell phone to call and we went to wait just at the mouth of the alley.

"It's only ten minutes," Dionne said. "You don't need to watch me."

"Dionne, there are drunks around, and it's not late, but this neighborhood isn't safe after dark." I could hear the loud conversation coming from down the street. Nothing violent, but I knew it could change quickly. "I don't want you to get hurt."

"Who's that?" Dionne asked.

I didn't need sight to know the answer. The chill of death and a faint echo of cries of grief were all I needed. "The Morrigan."

"Quinn and your friends. A beautiful night, isn't it?" As she spoke, I felt the temperature rise. Lionel blew air out and ended on a cough.

"Cool," Dionne said. "Is that a spell? Can I learn it?"

I had a vision of Dionne controlling the male population of her high school by exuding the essence of a fertility goddess. "No, not a spell. It's who she is." I hoped the taxi wouldn't show up while The Morrigan was around. It could, at minimum, cause a crash. "What can I do for you, Morrigan?"

"I require nothing from you this time, Quinn Larson. I come with information."

The heat fled replaced with a bone chilling cold. Two drunken men stumbled past, talking loudly, and reeking of beer. "Wow, did you see that crow? It was the size of a freaking buzzard."

"You're drunk. There wasn't a crow there. Come on. 'Scuse me, dude," the second man said after bumping me.

They passed the alley and seemed to have forgotten what they'd seen. "I appreciate the help, Morrigan. We are waiting for a taxi. Can you share this information before it arrives?"

A caw answered me. It turned into a spine sizzling laugh as she shifted from crow to woman. "I have watched your dance with the human world, wizard. You have been lucky until now. I do not know how long that will last."

"A prediction?"

"No, I see nothing in your future. Do not let that cause you concern. I do not think it's because you have no future."

A relief, but I was still worried that the cab would arrive before she finished with me. "I'll try not to worry about it."

"I have news about the six." Her silky voice seemed to caress me. I think she took my blindness as a challenge. Testing her power against my lack of sight was like a game, and she was winning. "Another has been born. Now there are four."

I couldn't help but think I'd started something when I uncovered the fact that Dionne was one of the six. The prophecy had been dormant for years and now it was cropping up everywhere. "Do you know who it is?"

"No, this news came to me in whispers on the wind. I feel the truth in the whispers, but no other knowledge came with it. It does not please me that something blocks my access to this truth."

Should I follow up on that last bit? Something powerful enough to block her was scary. "Thank you for bringing it to me." I wasn't ready to interrogate her just yet.

"You will find a way to show your appreciation, Quinn Larson, do not worry. Now, I think your taxi is arriving. Take care of the girl and this fairy." A breath of air rushed from the alley. A flap of wings just past my cheek and The Morrigan was gone.

"I totally need to know more about her," Dionne said.

"That means you'll have to study the history of the Real Folk," Lionel said. "Here's the cab."

"I promise I'll hit the books as soon as the inspection is over. Who was she again?"

"Later," I said. "We'll go over it tomorrow."

"Can we start with her?"

Would I ever get control of this apprentice? "Yes, as soon as you sit down to study, we'll start with the elementals."

"Okay, great. I'll see you tomorrow, early to set us up for the visit."

I heard a car door slam and Lionel call goodbye.

"Okay. Let's get going. I'm about ready to call it a day." My days were mainly about training apprentices with the occasional visit to Banks', all times when I was supposed to be in charge. Today had strained my patience at every step.

"Quinn Larson?" Bud whispered in my ear.

"Yes, Bud?" I was proud that she'd been quiet while The Morrigan was there.

"I think The Morrigan needs to learn to count. There were two of the six and if one more has been found, that makes three."

8

I couldn't put it off any longer. I was going to have to tell Bud about Dionne. "Lionel, let's get going. We'll talk as we go and take Bud home first."

We walked along the waterfront with Bud hidden under a conceal charm. She was too big now to simply hide under my jacket. It would look to anyone as though I was talking to Lionel the whole time. Being in a busy human area was a good way to avoid being overheard, because they seemed to prefer to concentrate on their own affairs.

"Lionel, keep an eye out for listeners while I tell Bud what she needs to know."

"Take my elbow so I don't have to pay attention to where you are." I felt his elbow bump my hand and slid my arm around his. Then Bud scrambled up my coat to sit on my shoulder. Fairies were light at full size, but a few more days and she'd be too big to just sit there unnoticed, too.

"You have a secret, Quinn Larson? I promise to keep it for you." Her hand grasped my ear for balance.

"Your oath takes care of that," I said. "I want you to think about the implications when I tell you this secret. This is a test of your leadership."

"Yes, Quinn Larson. I expect everything to be a test. Tell me the secret, please." Her breath tickled my ear. It felt like she was going to crawl into my brain and pull the information out in her eagerness.

"This secret is about Dionne, please let me or Lionel tell her that you know the secret. I promise we will do it as soon as possible."

"Yes, Quinn Larson, I will. Now tell me before I explode."

"Patience is something a leader needs to have," Lionel said. "Let Quinn tell it in his own way."

I was going to have to talk to Lionel about his tone. Bud might be annoying him, but she was going to be the leader of a prominent fairy tribe. He needed to show more respect, and I needed to stop thinking about talking to him and actually do it.

"We are almost home," Bud said. "You must tell me now or stop walking."

"Yes. You know we are researching the prophecy of the six."

"I know that, Quinn Larson. What is the secret?"

It was difficult to just blurt it out with the humans around. "Do you think there is a reason for that?"

"Because you think the prophecy will come true soon, and you want to know what will happen."

"Why would I think the prophecy is about to come true?"

"Wizards know things. Why are you asking all of these questions? Tell me the secret now."

We were close to the park and it sounded like there were only a few joggers nearby. "It is because Dionne is one of the six."

Silence for a few minutes. We were at the entrance to the park, and I wanted to avoid going in. Visiting with anyone who we bumped into would consume hours that we didn't have.

"Now I understand what The Morrigan meant. Quinn Larson, does Dionne know how powerful she is?"

"No. But that is because she was raised by humans. We need to help her understand her new world and prepare her for the prophecy." Lionel pulled my arm gently to stop me going farther. I heard the fountain in Lost Lagoon. We could slip around the side of the park and get home quickly. "We need to find out everything about the prophecy without alerting anyone about who she is."

"Yes. If people knew she was one of the prophesied, and that she didn't know our world, she would be in danger." Bud tweaked my ear. "I will think on this, Quinn Larson."

I opened my mouth to speak, but she pinched my ear. "Do not worry. I will not ask too many questions."

I felt her weight leave my shoulder. "Don't be late tomorrow." A giggle was all I got in response.

"Let's get home," Lionel said. "I expect we'll be doing research into the early hours."

It would help if we knew where to start. "I knew that there was always some of the six in existence. But now we have four. I don't think they are all here in Vancouver. I am afraid we are going to have to plan to travel with Dionne. That's not going to work if she is under the care of the government."

"I hadn't even considered that," Lionel's words came out on a groan. "I guess we need to hope this is going to take at least until she's eighteen. Do you know when her birthday is?"

"No. But we don't have any control over when the prophecy comes. I'm sure we'll figure something out." I wasn't, but I think it's important for the teacher to sound confident.

Lionel slowed his pace. "Uh, Quinn, the druids are waiting in our yard."

Damn. Why couldn't they just trust me to do my part? "We're going to have to work that out. They can't keep hanging around. It will cause some problems with the neighbors." And that could translate into problems with Ms. Metcalfe.

I led the way to the living room and plunked myself down on

the couch. I wasn't feeling hospitable and didn't care to pretend. I figured that, for now, the druids needed more from me than I did from them.

"Why were you waiting for me? I won't be able to do my part if I have to worry about you lurking on my doorstep. I have human neighbors, and they get curious." Not quite true. Most of my neighbors didn't care what I did as long as it didn't disturb the peace. The others were kept quiet with a gentle *ignore me* spell. It didn't stop me worrying, but it took the edge off.

"It is not our habit to wander the streets. If we cannot wait for you, perhaps you can give us access to your front hall."

"Not a chance."

"Then we will need a way to contact you when we have something to say." This time the voice was familiar, Myrddin.

"I don't understand why you feel the need to contact me. I will send Lionel to tell you when Fionuir is released. Unless you don't need to be advised."

"Yes, the souls will know. Today, we have news about the souls, information you need."

I tried to control the grouchiness. My head told me I was making things more difficult than they needed to be. But I was bone tired, and I'd had enough of people throwing barriers, or more problems, in my way. "Just tell me. I'll decide if I need this news."

"The souls have communicated with us. It is imperative that you release Fionuir as soon as possible."

"This is not new."

The druid whisper happened for a few minutes. I was about to ask them to finish and leave when Myrddin spoke. "It is not new information, you are correct. The level of urgency has increased. This task will not wait many more days. Perhaps all we have is a few hours."

I wanted to ask what they expected to happen if I didn't release her in time for whatever the souls had planned, but I realized I didn't need the information. I just needed to get them out of the house so we could focus on making some headway on all the tasks and problems. "I have met with Maeve and she has agreed to accept the responsibility for Fionuir. We have only to arrange for this to happen."

"Then you will complete the release tonight." This outburst came from my left. It seemed that Myrddin was not going to be the only one speaking.

"No. There are arrangements to be made. I promise that I will not delay more than needed."

"We must trust that you will keep your word, Quinn Larson," Myrddin said. "You have a reputation for fulfilling your promises. Now we will leave, and you must summon me as soon as you have arranged for the release."

It was time to try to collect on our agreement. "Before you leave, I need information on the prophecy of the six."

The druids started to whisper among themselves. I waited patiently, but I felt Lionel fidget beside me. "Be still. It is not going to hurt." I hoped that was true.

The whispering stopped. I wondered if we could find a spell that allowed us to have a conversation no one would be able to hear no matter how close.

"We agreed to the price of information when you upheld your side. If we provide you with information and you are not successful in releasing the sidhe, we will require payment. We have previously provided you with the ability to save one life. Would you return it?"

That was too valuable. I needed to take a risk – not too much of one since I was sure I could release Fionuir. "I will owe you a service if I should fail."

More whispers, then Myrddin said, "Accepted. I will remain to provide you with the information we have on the prophecy while my brothers leave."

I nodded. "If I have information you do not on the prophecy, what price will you pay?"

"Listen to Myrddin before you try to sell us information, wizard." The voice was harsh, making me wonder if they had heard The Morrigan's news.

When we were alone again, Myrddin accepted a mug of tea and cleared his throat. I wasn't sure how I felt about a nervous druid, but then again, maybe he was uncomfortable without the other two. I don't remember ever seeing a druid without at least one companion.

"Before I tell you our knowledge of the prophecy, I must insist you agree not to share it with any others. If one of the six should learn what the prophecy means, it would have dire results."

So, they didn't know the identity of the six. I wasn't going to give them that piece of information. Although it occurred to me that it was odd that they didn't need to research anything, that the information was to hand. "Would you prefer that Lionel left?"

"No, that is not necessary, but do not share it with your other apprentices. They may not have the discipline to understand the importance of this information."

Lionel sputtered. "The apprentice oath will prevent them from sharing secrets."

I held up my hand to stop him continuing. "I will decide what my apprentice hears from me." I had no desire to let Dionne in on her fate until we needed to, and Bud would not need to know the prophecy to lead the Rose tribe. I nodded and gestured for him to continue.

"Let us start with some background. The prophecy states that six Real Folk with the full five powers will one day exist at the same time in our world."

"Yes," Lionel said. "We have been able to find out that."

I held up my hand to caution him about sharing too much of what we knew. "Continue, Myrddin. We will not interrupt again."

"We will not know who the six are, or rather who they all are, until they meet. But the first time the sixth one touches all of the powers, the final stages will begin, and the six will journey to their meeting place."

I wished I hadn't promised not to interrupt. I bit down on the questions that bubbled in the back of my mind until he had finished.

"A hundred years ago, five of the six existed. The sixth did not come to being, and so the prophecy did not happen. This time, we think there are already three existing in this time. Our history tells us that when the number reaches five, there is a time limit. Either the sixth is discovered, or the five die within two years."

The thought of losing Dionne brought back the pain of Cate's death. I swallowed and wished for something hopeful. Maybe that fulfilling the prophecy would be better than having them die. Although, with ancient prophecies, there was no guarantee that it would be a boon to the world.

"Now," Myrddin continued as though giving a lecture. "The actual prophecy is shrouded in mystery. There are rumors that it is dependent on the world when it comes to fruition. That should it happen today, it would be different from what would have occurred fifty years in the past or would occur fifty years in the future. But no matter when it happens, change will come to the Real Folk. We know that change brings confusion, and panic, and conflict as often as it brings good."

This was nothing new, but it was good to hear confirmation at least. Thinking he was finished, I decided to start asking questions. "How do you know that there is a time limit for the sixth?"

"Occasionally we have known who hold the five powers. In the ancient times when we lived in our homeland, in a time when people, humans and Real Folk, would look to the druids for training and knowledge. Twice our records show us that this has happened."

If he was so forthcoming with information, I guessed the

druids needed me for something other than releasing Fionuir. "How do the six know where to meet?"

"They will know. I don't like to guess, but perhaps the sixth brings a way for them to communicate."

I couldn't think of any other questions, so I indicated to Lionel that he was free to ask until Myrddin pulled the plug.

"Is there a sign that we will know the six are born?" he asked as though he had a list.

"There is mention of a sign, but we have not been able to find details."

"What if they are not trained? If one of them is a child?" He had been thinking this through.

"We have no information on that," Myrddin said.

"When the final one comes into their power, or is born, do you know if there is a period when they must meet?"

"No, that is not written and since this prophecy has not yet come to pass, there is only our supposition. To the best of my knowledge, there have never been six."

"Do you think they need to be together physically to make the prophecy happen?"

"That is a good question. You will be a good student when you take advantage of the time we have agreed to give you. Now I think we have reached the end of our story. I must return to the museum."

"Why won't you answer that question, Myrddin?" If he was hiding something, it could be vital. Or it could just be that he was tired of answering questions.

"It seems we do not know enough about the prophecy to satisfy the thirst of apprentices. I must return to the museum. I am not happy to be separated from my brothers."

We had been allowed to ask more questions than I expected. But now the door had been closed on the prophecy information, I needed to know about the amulet. Fionuir had used it as power battery, keeping the fairies from breeding unless they stole the life force of humans. I'd cleaned the spell from it before sending Fionuir away. The souls hadn't seemed disturbed when I returned the amulet to the druids, but I wondered why the druids kept them trapped.

"Before you leave, Myrddin, I am curious about the amulet."

"I have not been authorized to provide you with any information about the souls. I do not think I would be given such permission. Or if I am, the price may be more than you are prepared to pay."

That wasn't a surprise, but my question wasn't really about the souls themselves. "I was just wondering why the souls are kept within the amulet. Surely some way can be found to release them and allow them to rest permanently."

"Why should I answer these questions, wizard. Do you think I am weakened without my brothers here?"

I was walking a thin line, but they needed me to help, so maybe I still had a bit of leeway. "It may make a difference to how I advise Maeve on containing Fionuir. She seems to be linked to the souls in some way."

"She used the amulet and that is what links them. The link should be broken when she is returned to this plane."

It had been worth a try. Before I could wish him safe trip back to the museum, he continued, "If we released them to other vessels, it may also break that connection. But what would be the difference? They are, at least, not alone in the amulet."

Interesting, he didn't consider that the souls would be happier if they were allowed to pass to the next existence. "Do you mean you could transfer them to other vessels?" My curiosity pulled my imagination along.

"A soul can be placed in any inanimate object or can share the body of another soul for a very short time. This is elementary information, Quinn Larson. I am surprised that you need to ask."

Not everyone studied magic that affected the dead.

Summoning spirits for information was the extent of my knowledge. "What do the souls do in there?"

"Why are you so interested, Quinn Larson? We have not agreed to provide you with information on any subject you find interesting. Do you wish to negotiate with us for more? You need to do so formally."

I'd hit a nerve. My suspicion was that the souls were restless because of the prophecy. "I was just curious. It is not important. Thank you for your information, Myrddin. We will let you know when we are ready to release Fionuir."

"Good night, Quinn Larson. Lionel, I look forward to the time when you join us for your training."

I heard a murmured conversation as Lionel escorted the druid to the door.

"What was that about?" I asked when Lionel rejoined me.

"We were discussing what I would focus on when I started my study hours. I don't have much time so he told me to do some deep thinking on what I would like to accomplish. Why did you ask about the souls being placed in another container?"

I couldn't say for sure what prompted the questions, but now I was more curious than ever. "I don't like the idea that someone would spend eternity in something like the amulet. It strikes me as a prison. It didn't seem to occur to Myrddin that they could be released to the next life."

He cleared the mugs and washed them before joining me. "I would not like to be there. When I pass to the next life, I want to wander the world and collect information on everything. If you think it's important, I could use my time with the druids researching the magic of the amulet."

"No. That time is yours. You should learn something you are interested in, not something for me. If I find myself driven by the question, I'll arrange for my own time with them." I made a protective sign in the air to ward me from any circumstance that made me need the druids for information.

9

Bud arrived on time for a change, and we spent the day alternating between trying to get her to stop asking questions about Dionne and having her study some history of her tribe. My plan had been to get her to understand where mistakes had been made in the past and discuss how she would do things differently. By the time Dionne arrived, my temper was starting to fray. Lionel had retreated to his room after his last spat with Bud over the idea that she might be one of the six. Fairies didn't test for their power until they were past childhood, so she could be, but every part of me hoped it wasn't true. We'd find out in a few months, I guess.

"I've got an idea of what your business could be," Dionne announced as she charged into the living room. "It could really be a business too. You could pay me."

"Dionne, I missed you!" The clatter of a saucer accompanied Bud's words. "I have learned many things. And I was teaching Quinn how to make fairy tea. And there is so much history for me to learn."

I held up my hand in caution, hoping she would remember that she couldn't tell Dionne about the prophecy. Her oath would stop her speaking, but there could be a lag. Bud being cut off in the middle of a sentence would do as much to pique Dionne's interest as the actual news.

"Oh, don't worry, Quinn Larson, I know some things are secret. But I do know your secret, Dionne," Bud's voice took on an awed tone. "You are one of the six."

I heard Dionne take in a breath. "I thought we had to keep this between us."

And Bud was supposed to let us tell Dionne that we'd shared her secret. "Bud can be trusted, Dionne. She cannot tell anyone. Now what's the business?"

"I found this cool affiliate site. I know you already have one, but this one works differently." She proceeded to explain a complicated Internet business that seemed to run all on its own. I wasn't clear how it was different from what I was already doing.

"You'll need to tell me how I explain this to Ms. Metcalfe, but it sounds fine to me. Now we've got a bit of time for lessons before she arrives. Bud, please ask Lionel to join us."

I heard a tiny hiss of frustration, but then she knocked on his door.

I dug into my pocket and pulled out a couple of acorns. "One of these has a spell inside and the other does not. Dionne, you need to figure out which is which, what the spell is, and then recreate it on the blank."

"How am I supposed to start?" Her voice was just bordering on a whine. "This would be a lot easier if I lived here and could spend more time on magic."

I couldn't get into that discussion with Ms. Metcalfe on her way over. We only had about an hour before Bud would have to hide, and we'd have to pretend to be human. There was time for one lesson, maybe two if she was quick, and didn't whine too much. "Start by feeling out the two acorns. If you can't figure it out, we'll give you some clues."

There was a pause then she dropped one of the acorns into my hand. "Okay this is the one with the spell. I think it's some kind of sound charm."

"You were very fast," Bud said. "Is she right, Quinn Larson?"

I nodded. "Now figure out the exact noise and recreate the spell." Usually an apprentice studied for months before trying this lesson. I wasn't surprised that she'd identified which one had the charm, that was easy, but she'd almost identified the exact spell. Her combination of powers must be helping her gain knowledge. The charm held the sound of approaching help; running feet and a few calls of 'stop' and 'hey'.

Dionne sighed. "Lionel, will you help me?"

I wanted to tell her to work it out herself, but Lionel needed to learn how to say no to her. And it didn't matter at this point. The spells were simple, and she'd have lessons when Lionel wasn't around, so eventually she'd have to do it herself.

He surprised me. "I can help by making the sounds, but you need to figure out how to create the spell. You know everything you need, Dionne, don't doubt yourself."

"You should help her, Lionel," Bud's voice squeaked. "She is special and shouldn't have to spend time figuring out simple things."

I heard Lionel's sigh and decided to step in before the bickering began in earnest. "Bud, we need to talk about your lessons. Let's go to the living room and leave these two to the kitchen."

She took my hand and followed me to the couch. "What lesson am I to learn today?"

I decided to take her compliance at face value and pushed away the images in my mind of her making faces at me. "Sometimes when you are a leader, you need to make people do things they don't want to do or deny them what they want."

"Like Dionne," she said. "She has to learn in case you, or Lionel, are not there when she needs to cast a spell."

"Yes, but you are right that she doesn't have time to figure out simple things. How would you solve this problem?"

"It is a hard question. I do not know what you can do. If I have to solve this... I know! I would find a spell that would give her some of the simple information. Then she would only have to learn how to do the difficult things. Is that a good answer, Quinn Larson?"

If there were a spell like that, it would be the right answer. "There is no spell like that."

"I would make her learn. But that means I will not be able to talk with her and play with her. It is not fair to me."

"Yes, it is not fair, but it is much more important that Dionne learn in the precious time we have with her, than play with you."

Before we could say anything more, I heard a giggle from Dionne and a yell from Lionel. "Is everything okay?"

"One second," Dionne called.

I dreaded the silence, but it only took a second before I felt Dionne drop an acorn in my hand. "Here, I think I've done it."

I sought the spell and it seemed to be right. "How does it trigger?"

"You scratch it," Dionne answered.

"And how do you stop it?"

"I didn't know I had to stop it. It will just go once and then it's done."

"Lionel?"

He cleared his throat, and I guess he hadn't thought to help her place restrictions. "It's a single shot. I'll teach her on-off spells after this."

I scratched the acorn with my nail and suddenly the house was filled with giggles and shouts of 'stop'. Far from being a single shot, the sounds got louder, and it felt like an attack, the giggles rising to shrieks and the yells feeling like physical blows.

"I'm sorry," Dionne yelled over the barrage of sound. "How do we stop it?"

I put the acorn on the floor and gestured for someone to

stomp on it. The sound cut off. The silence was broken by a banging from the door.

"Ms. Metcalfe," Lionel whispered.

"Bud, downstairs," I pointed to the door. "You can browse the books. Lionel, go let her in. Dionne, can you cover up the mess of the acorn?"

"I can pull the rug over it," she said with a grunt. "Okay, clean. Now do you remember what I told you about the business?"

"Enough to fool her, maybe. You can answer any of the more difficult questions."

"Mr. Larson, what was that noise? Is someone hurt?" Ms. Metcalfe was on full defense of the innocent mode.

"No. We were testing some sound effects for the website," Dionne answered for me. "I think they need to be toned down. Don't you?"

"Indeed. Now let us get on with this inspection. Where is your office space?"

I didn't like the idea of a human wandering my home when I couldn't cast any protective spells. I couldn't let my feelings get in the way. It would only take a few minutes, and then we'd be safe. "Dionne, please make some tea for us while we go to the office." I reached out to where I thought Ms. Metcalfe stood and tried to sound welcoming. "There's not much to see, Ms. Metcalfe. Lionel, please lead the way."

We went upstairs to the empty room and I gave my practiced speech. "The furniture is on order. Until it arrives, Dionne will work downstairs. I'll have the computers set up tomorrow."

There was silence. I tried not to add any information into the void. Ms. Metcalfe tapped one of the boxes. "The space is quite large. Will you have other employees?"

"Not right away, but we may expand in the future."

I heard Lionel shuffling a box aside. "We'll send most of this to storage," he said. "You can see there's a window here. We'll set up a coffee station over here and the washroom is downstairs."

Dionne must have coached him as well. "Do you have any questions?" I hoped not. If she wanted to get into the details of the business, I'd run out of information after a few sentences.

"Only about Dionne's duties, and we can do that downstairs. I suggest you get a fan up here it is quite stuffy."

I assured her we would, but I knew a spell would work so much better than a fan. Great, now I was thinking like we'd be using the space for business. It was a good spell for Dionne to learn though. "The tea will be ready."

I followed them down the stairs and heard Dionne placing cups on the kitchen counter. She offered Ms. Metcalfe honey and then poured the tea.

I heard a sip and then the questions started, "Now, Dionne, tell me what you'll be doing for Mr. Larson."

I tensed. If she didn't get this right, we'd be under scrutiny all the time.

"I'll be doing some general office work for the most part, Ms. Metcalfe. The business is mostly on-line, but I'll need to answer questions and help people with problems when we're up and running."

That sounded innocent enough. I tried not to sigh out the tension.

Dionne continued, "I'll be helping set up the website at first. It's not a hard job but it takes a lot of concentration."

"That's a lot of responsibility. I hope you are learning something while you are helping." There was a weight of suspicion in her voice.

"I'll be teaching Dionne basic business skills," I said, hoping she wouldn't want details.

"And will she be able to keep up her schoolwork?"

"I will make sure she has enough time to get her studying done." It wouldn't be schoolwork she was studying, but it would be study.

"I can tutor her," Lionel said. "Once we get up and running, I can make sure she gets an hour of study every time she works in the office. That should keep her on track."

Ms. Metcalfe sniffed; I hoped it was the tea, not her disbelief. "Well, that sounds fine. I will need to do periodic checks, but I think Dionne is in good hands. Thank you for taking her on."

I kept the relief off my face and hoped that Lionel and Dionne did too. "I'm sure she'll work hard."

"I will, but I have a question, Ms. Metcalfe."

"What is it, Dionne."

"It would be great if we could get this up and running fast. What would we need to do so I could stay overnight? On the weekend, like, it wouldn't interfere with school. It would probably only be once."

I wished I had the power to wind time back. That one question could undo all the progress we'd made. There was no sound. No clue for me as to the reaction. I didn't know whether to speak, stay quiet, or to just pass out.

Finally, Ms. Metcalfe responded, "I don't think that's a good idea, Dionne."

"But—"

I interrupted before she did any more damage. "Dionne, you don't have to work through the weekend. We will be fine on the current schedule."

"Why would you need to stay through the night?" Ms. Metcalfe didn't sound happy.

"There's a lot of work. I just thought..."

"Staying alone in a house with two men isn't a good idea. I thought you would be more careful than that."

"It's not two men, its Quinn and Lionel." She stopped. "I mean, they are men, but they aren't strangers."

"What do you think your foster parents would think of the idea?"

I could hear the weight of the threat in the words. "They are aware of her job."

"I'm sure they are, Mr. Larson."

"I was just thinking, don't worry. I won't be staying overnight." Dionne was clearly trying to repair the damage.

"I think I need to schedule a home visit soon, Dionne. Now let us talk about the working arrangements."

"I will make sure she is home at a reasonable time during the week. Her entire weekend will not be spent working in our office, I promise. I understand she has agreed to do volunteer work on weekends anyway."

A quiet huff filled the gap after my words. "Indeed, Mr. Larson. I expect work won't stop if Dionne isn't here."

"She is a great help, but yes, we will continue to survive without her." I gave her a smile, hoping she'd take the joke and drop any suspicion. "If other teenagers were as responsible as Dionne, the world would be a better place."

"You may be right, Mr. Larson. Well, let us leave it at that. I must be going. Thank you for the tea. I'll let you know when the next visit needs to be scheduled."

I had to know if Dionne's question had caused problems, but I couldn't make it worse. "I hope our business will be up and running before the next visit. I can't help but think your time here has been wasted."

"Not at all. I am comfortable with the environment you have for her. You are right, because the office isn't set up, I'll need to come back next week to confirm the actual environment."

Weekly meetings would not be a good thing. There were too many things to juggle to have this repeated. What would happen if she came snooping around when we were bringing Fionuir back? "Would it help if we contacted you when the desks arrived? That way you know your visit will be a valuable use of your time."

"That would be helpful, yes. I will still be scheduling visits, Mr. Larson. I take my responsibility seriously. Is there any reason I wouldn't be welcome?"

A million reasons. "Not at all. I know you want to make sure

Dionne is in a good environment. I look forward to your next visit." *Like I look forward to a plague of locusts.*

Lionel escorted Ms. Metcalfe to the door and I held onto my words until I knew we were safely alone.

"Dionne, I said not to make her suspicious – to be careful. If you can't keep things simple, we'll never get you trained." I wasn't yelling. I kept control of my temper by reminding myself she was a teenager and prone to impulsive behavior. Or at least that was how human teenagers acted and she was as close to human as she could get right now.

"Don't fret, she'll be cool." Dionne didn't sound at all worried. I opened my mouth to respond, but she just kept talking. "I know it looks like it, but she doesn't really care about me. I'm just a file to her, and as long as I don't cause trouble, she'll be cool."

"That's too big a risk. You can't do that again. If you can't control yourself, I'll make sure you are not here for any further meetings."

I heard Lionel mutter something, then Bud piped up with, "I think you are right, Lionel. That was as silly as my mistake was, Dionne. Come, Lionel, we have something to do."

I sensed them leave in the silence that fell between Dionne and me. Lionel was giving me – or maybe Dionne – some privacy so we could straighten something out.

"Dionne, you are my apprentice, and you need to listen to my instructions. I may not know about the way humans live, but I know how to avoid getting into trouble with them." I waited for some response. I hoped for some understanding of what she'd done. But I'd settle for an apology.

"But, Quinn, I need you to train me. I need to learn. If I can only do this in a few hours a week, we'll never get me ready." Now her voice carried panic.

I patted the sofa beside me and waited until I felt her sit. "You will be ready, don't worry. Even if the prophecy actually comes to play this time, we have years." I hoped we did anyway.

"How can you know that? I need to learn five different kinds of magic. And I need to learn about everything you all know by just living in this world." I didn't have to see to know she was on the edge of tears.

"First of all, you don't need to learn everything five times. You learn magic, and then you can spend time exploring the differences."

She blew out air. "That's a relief. Okay, I'm sorry. It just feels like we're not getting anywhere. I thought if I was here for a weekend, we could make some progress."

I couldn't let her off the hook. "So, you thought you would just ignore my instructions and do things the way you want to, regardless of the consequences?"

"I said I was sorry. I am. I promise I won't do it again."

Could I hold her to that promise? Her apprentice oath should have kept her from asking the question in the first place. "Did you feel anything when you asked her?"

"Like what? You think someone made me ask? No, I wanted to know. I thought about it all day."

"When you asked the question, did you feel anything?"

"No, nothing. Should I have felt something?"

I would have to test her vows. If they hadn't taken, I would have to find another way to keep her from trouble. "I don't know. Your promise should be enough. A promise from an apprentice to a teacher is binding. Think about how you would tell her what is really going on here."

"I can't. Like, I'm trying, but the words won't form."

That was a relief. "Okay, don't worry about it, that's what should happen. Let's hope Ms. Metcalfe doesn't decide to keep a closer eye on your job."

"Can't you just cast a spell on her so she'll forget about what I said? Hey maybe she can forget that she should check up on us. Then we'll be fine."

I reminded myself she didn't grow up with us. She had to be

told the simplest things. Magic was the least of her lessons. "Casting spells on humans isn't simple. They are complex creatures, and any spell can backfire. It's considered unethical to use magic on them. I think it's more about surviving any fallout than any real moral concern."

"But you all cast glamours. That is magic cast on humans."

"No, it's cast on the person you want to conceal. If we tried to change Ms. Metcalfe's memory of your question, we could erase her memory of her job, or her home, or her family. We don't know how she associates things in her mind."

"Fine, I won't ask any more questions, I promise. Now can we get some more training done before I have to leave?"

"There are two histories I need you to read first. Then tomorrow, we'll change our focus to your magic training. Get Lionel to give you our records of the witch trials and the vampire killings."

"I learned about the witch trials in school."

"No, you learned the human truth of it. This is our side, our truth. I know I mentioned it before, but now you need to read it." It might give her a better understanding of why we needed to hide.

"I never heard of vampire killings. I thought vampires were fiction."

"Just read what Lionel gives you."

10

L ionel and Bud came out of his room as soon as Dionne gave them the all clear. No one talked about what had just happened, I guess they decided I should handle it without interference – or help.

Ten minutes, later Dionne was reading the books that Lionel brought up from the workroom. Bud, Lionel, and I were plotting out the next few days of spells.

"I know you have to prepare for Fionuir's release," Lionel said. "Maybe I can do some basic training for Dionne and then you can concentrate on one thing."

"Yes, Quinn Larson, let Lionel train Dionne and we can practice being leaders." Bud placed her hand on my knee. "My mother is expecting me to be able to pass a test the tribe will create."

Another deadline, great! "When is that?"

"It will be soon, I think. But I will know before the test. Perhaps they will provide an invitation for you to attend."

I had a faint memory of when I felt in control of my life. "Okay, so tomorrow we start with a plan. I will have some spells set up with Lionel to train Dionne, and some ideas of how we get you prepared to pass your leadership test – now, a little peace."

A cackle of laughter cut off my hope for some quiet time. "Lionel, is that The Morrigan?"

"You don't need to ask him," the harsh voice was right beside my ear.

How had she slipped past my wards? "I don't remember inviting you in."

"Ah, you don't remember everything you say to me, Quinn. But you did once say words that I understood to be invitation." The voice slipped into the heat that was the fertility goddess. I heard Lionel take deep breaths. I wondered how it was affecting Dionne. There was no sound from her or Bud.

"I don't wish to seem rude, but this visit is the only one I agree to. I will have my privacy."

"I will not take offense this time, wizard." Her breath was warm on my ear. "I have news."

I swallowed and thought about icebergs. The Morrigan chuckled and hot shivers chased through my blood.

"There is little time. Another of the six has found their power. That leaves only one more to be discovered. Train this one fast, Quinn. I feel change icing the wind."

The weight on my lap disappeared. I felt the bite of talons on my thigh and then the breeze of wings. Dionne said, "Oh wow," in a hushed tone.

The Morrigan cawed and the sound was accompanied by the stench of carrion.

My hope that The Morrigan was finished was dashed when I heard a keening. No earthly crow could make that sound. The pain of a thousand battles tore at my soul while she continued.

I felt tiny fingers touch my hand. "Don't fear, Quinn Larson," Bud whispered. "I will not let her harm anyone."

A trickle of humor lightened the bleakness that had seeped into my bones. "Thank you, Bud."

Dionne sucked in a breath and I hoped she would recover.

Sending her home depressed was not going to endear us to her family. Lionel was silent.

"I have more." The Morrigan had switched back to woman and the ice in the room melted. "You are too trusting, wizard."

"I have no reason to mistrust someone, why would I?"

"You are blind to the truth when it is in front of your eyes. You trust those who will harm you, and you step close to the line with me."

It wasn't smart to argue with someone as powerful as The Morrigan, but I was too tired of hints and insinuations. "Who are you warning me against? I am not going to suspect everyone in my life just on the off chance one of them is lying."

"There will always be liars in your life, Quinn Larson." I felt heavy silk slither across my neck. She was stalking me. Caressing my senses along with my skin. Part of me longed to pull her onto my lap. The other part wished she would put me out of my misery.

"I'm not a child. I know people lie. You wouldn't be here to tell me about normal behavior. Something, or someone, is lying about something important. Now, please tell me what you came to say and let me get back to what I was doing." I held my breath, but no smiting happened. Lionel finally made some noise. I think he was trying to say my name, but it just came out as a choking cough.

"Many people lie about important things. Maeve is considering her own gain in what you are doing. The druids are not telling you what you should know."

"That is always true of the druids." I was sure there were secrets the druids kept that had no importance. I knew that I had to be careful in any agreement with them.

"Do not get comfortable with your ability to see the lies within the truth. Too much is at stake. Not everything is as you hope it to be."

Bud's hand squeezed my finger, and I held back on my

response. The Morrigan had her own agenda, and I would never feel safe around her no matter how much she pretended to help me. "Thank you for the warning. I will take care. If you have any information about the change the prophecy will bring, you are welcome into my home."

A warm laugh plucked at the nerves in my spine. "Well spoken, wizard. Goodnight."

The room froze and then warmed.

"She is gone, Quinn Larson," Bud said, patting my hand. "I told you I would not let her hurt you."

"Oh my God," Dionne said. "She is so cool. Can I learn that?"

Lionel beat me to the answer. "No, it's not a magic you can learn. She is magic."

"Yes, and a bossy one." Bud patted my hand one more time. "I think I must return to my tribe. Will you be safe if I leave?"

"Yes, Bud, thank you. Please be careful going home. Dionne, I think you should head home too." There were too many things I needed to think through. If they left, it would mean no one would be adding to the list.

As soon as we were alone, Lionel asked, "How do you argue with The Morrigan? I can barely breathe when she is around. It doesn't seem to matter what aspect she shows, I'm either terrified, or, well terrified I guess, just in a different way."

I rubbed my forehead trying to erase a sudden pressure. "It isn't easy, but I've had more experience than you. And it is a little easier when you can't see her. And I think she likes me." I was going for levity, but it rang true.

"I'm not sure that's a good thing."

"Having an elemental like you?"

"Yeah, what if she decides she doesn't one day?"

That sent a new chill through me. "I'll keep it in mind."

He shuffled something on the table. "I'm worried, Quinn. We don't have long to train Dionne. What about trying to get permission for her to stay. I know you told her it was too dangerous, but it's more dangerous for her to be untrained."

He had a point, but I had to maintain some control, and that meant keeping Dionne safe at home as long as possible. "Someone kept her safe all these years. We need to trust that will continue. There's still one more of the six to discover. If we can believe the druids, we have up to two years. And then the six have to start communicating."

"I'm not sure we have all that much time. There seems to be another one showing up every time we turn around."

I nodded. "I figure we have a few months at least. I hope we have a couple of years. She has a lot to learn."

"Maybe you should have asked The Morrigan who the others are. Maybe one is a baby? That would give us a long time to train Dionne."

"I'll see what I can do about getting that next time."

"Why do I feel like we don't get that kind of luck, that she's likely to say all the others are fully trained? Tea?"

My apprentice was sometimes wiser than me. "Yes, tea will do since there's nothing stronger."

The sound of water filling the kettle stopped. "You know, Quinn, I noticed Dionne doesn't seem too bound by her oath."

"Why do you think that is?" I could use any ideas Lionel came up with. I still wasn't comfortable with Dionne's ability to say things, or ask questions, regardless of my wishes.

"I've never met a wizard or witch with more than one power, but Cate told me about someone she knew, someone called Mika Blue? Did you know him?"

"I never met him, because he was an apprentice with her first master. What did she say about him?" I remembered feeling jealous. I hated hearing about how clever he was, and how quick he learned. And I always suspected he'd been more than a fellow apprentice with Cate. That still hurt now, even though... well it hurt.

"She said he would argue with their master. It was like his oath was looser. Maybe it only covers one power completely."

"I'm not sure that would make the difference."

"Can you test her?" He placed a mug of tea at my fingertips. "I mean make sure the oath holds."

"Think about a way to test her and we'll try, but I'm sure it's not the oath. I wonder if it's the influence of a human upbringing."

"What do you know about human teenagers?" I could hear the interest in his voice. "Is there some way to do research? I could go out and observe so we could compare it with what we know about wizards."

"It's a good idea, Lionel, but we have a lot to do right now. I think we can put off the research until we've dealt with Fionuir."

"But what if she says something to her foster parents?"

A tapping at the window drew my attention. "Lionel, check who's at the window and let them in. We'll continue with this later."

"It's Olan. He's coming around to the front."

Olan wasn't tall enough to knock the front door, so he got our attention at the back window. "It will be good to have a chat with an old friend."

"I'm not here for a chat, Quinn. You asked for me to look into the prophecy." I felt him climb the couch beside me. "Now, you know we pixies are all over the place. I'll tell you something you don't know about us, but I need you and Lionel to swear you won't tell anyone. I mean anyone."

I agreed. Olan waited until Lionel finished his oath swearing. He tended to the overly formal, but it seemed appropriate.

"Good. We pixies also communicate with each other no matter how far apart we are. I sent out a request for information on the six or the prophecy." He paused and I heard him smack his lips together. "I'd love a saucer of that tea, Lionel."

Like other pixies, Olan was a master storyteller. If he was

taking his time, I figured the information wasn't urgent, and I could enjoy the tale.

Lionel put my warm mug in my hand, and I heard a slurp from beside me.

"Ah, that's perfect. Now, I couldn't get any more information on the prophecy, but I found out about two of the six. They have started reaching out. My cousins in Bolivia know of a woman and my cousins in Wales know of a boy. Both of them have started asking the pixies about sending messages, but neither of them knows each other yet."

If they were trying to communicate with each other, then the prophecy was coming closer. I couldn't let Olan know what The Morrigan had told us; that until all of the six were available we could avoid this prophecy.

Lionel offered cookies, and then asked, "Do you know anything about the power of six. I mean the individual powers."

"They have all five, that's about all I know. And you know that too, what exactly are you asking, Lionel? What little detail of information are you trying to tie down?"

I nodded to Lionel. He wouldn't tell Olan about Dionne, but his question was good. Maybe knowing how she was able to get around her oath, and ask Ms. Metcalfe about a sleepover, would help keep her safe. And keep her from breaking it again.

Lionel asked, "I've been wondering how that works. Do you think they are stronger in one power? Like they are really an earth power with the rest being add-ons?"

"That's a good question. I can ask if anyone knows. It would be interesting if each was stronger in a different power, but that would mean there needed to be a sixth power. That's not possible. There are only five, earth, air, spirit, water, and fire."

I sipped at my tea and let the conversation continue.

"Yes, I guess that's true." Lionel paused again, and I heard Olan rustling beside me. Lionel continued, "I don't think there's a hidden power out there. Do your cousins know if the woman and the boy are apprenticed?"

"Yes, they are both apprenticed to fire wizards. Why?"

"It occurs to me that oaths might be tied to the power. Maybe if you have more powers, you need to take different oaths."

"That's new to me, Lionel. There are dual powers out there, but I've never heard of taking the apprentice oath more than one time with a master. The two I know about are still in training, and if their master wasn't able to hold the oath we would have heard. Why are you asking?"

Before Lionel could raise Olan's curiosity any further, I said, "It's tedious enough to take the oath once. What if they had to make sure they took the oath with their primary power?"

"How would you know that?" Lionel said before Olan could answer. "How would you know which of the powers was primary?"

Olan shifted beside me; I could almost feel his interest building. "I have no idea, Lionel. What has woken this interest in apprentice oaths? Are you trying to find a loophole?"

"No, I would never do that."

The affront in his voice almost made me laugh. The thought of his hurt feelings kept it inside. "Lionel is almost done with his apprenticeship. He doesn't need to find a loophole. He needs to learn to direct his curiosity."

Olan slurped his tea. "I never thought I'd hear a wizard say that curiosity was a bad thing."

"I said it needed to be directed. Lionel, I think you need to get back to your research." I hoped he wouldn't ask what I meant.

"Yes, Quinn. I'll just clean up the tea things. Can I get you anything else, Olan?"

"No, I'll be off. I have other things to do. Thank you again for the tea."

Lionel showed Olan to the door.

"Get some sleep," I said when he returned. "When we've

released Fionuir, I'll oversee your spell creation, and you can be released from the apprenticeship."

"You don't have to do that. I can still help you with Dionne and Bud."

"I hope you'll stay around after you graduate to full wizard. I will need your help, but I'll understand if you want to go out on your own."

"Are you kidding? Prophecies, The Morrigan, imprisoned sidhe princesses. Where else would I get all this excitement?"

"Excitement isn't all it's cracked up to be. But thanks, I still need your help getting around."

"As long as you need me, Quinn, I'll be here as long as you need me."

11

It was a rare peaceful morning. Lionel was still sleeping, and Bud wasn't due for an hour – if she managed to arrive on time. I had a chance to sit and think things over without any advice, asked for or not. I stirred a saucepan of leftover stew on the stove and made a pot of tea. The stew was rich with herbs and rabbit. It tasted like home and safety.

I pushed aside my feelings and tried to think about how to get past this constant demand on my life. It seemed like every time I got a handle on what I needed to do, I got slapped in the face with someone else's problems. It's not like it was a new situation. It had been happening since I saw the first dead human. Fionuir's actions had taken away what little control I thought I had over my life. Being blind was just the most obvious piece. I wouldn't feel sorry for myself. I got by okay without my sight.

Heating the stew didn't keep my attention long. I put the bowl on the table and sat down. Time to pretend I had control of my priorities.

So, first thing to do, Dionne's training. It was the easiest thing on my to-do list. I'd come to understand how to teach an apprentice with Lionel. Planning her training was easy, getting through it would be another matter. I could set up a series of spells starting with simple ones and then getting more complex until Lionel figured she was ready to do some independent study. I would still have to find a way to get her to learn some history, no, that was her influence. All of the history, just not all at once.

I hadn't had a lot of luck lately so maybe I was due. There was always a possibility we had years to train her. I tried not to think that the possibility was down to two options, slim and none.

I couldn't put off Fionuir's release for long. Maeve could change her mind. The druids wouldn't let me anyway. So maybe that would be the first priority. Or, the first after planning Dionne's education. Oh, yes, and Bud's although she was learning fast. If it was only about getting her confidence back after the fire incident, she'd be ready for the leadership test in a few days. Another thing I didn't know – when was the test?

I scraped the bowl hoping for one more mouthful, but it was empty ,and I wasn't really hungry, just wanting a bit of distraction. My tea was cooling and getting bitter. I took bowl and mug to the sink and left them for Lionel to clean up. We'd learned early on, at the price of more than a few cups and plates, that I couldn't manage to clean if I couldn't see.

The birds rose and began the morning chorus; the joyous songs lifting the cloud from my mind. A few minutes later, I heard Lionel stumbling around his room, so I put the kettle on and turned up the flame under the stew pot. One thing that all apprentices had in common was they woke up starving.

While Lionel shoveled his breakfast into his mouth, I told him what I'd decided.

He spoke through a mouthful of stew, "I think Dionne should learn some defense spells. After we figure out a way to make sure her oath sticks. Can you imagine what she'd do to someone she didn't like if she was able to cast a defense spell, and there were no restrictions on using it?"

He laughed, but I did imagine it and my stomach dropped at

the thought of Ms. Metcalfe asking if we'd shown Dionne how to... well whatever. "It might be faster to make a charm to block her magic when she's in the human world." I didn't know where that idea had come from, but it was a great solution. "She'd have to agree, but that shouldn't be a problem."

"Is there a spell for that?"

"Not exactly, but you can build on a shield spell. It will be good practice for creating your own."

He clomped over to the sink. "I've been doing some thinking about my spell. I think I'd like to make it something like a truth spell."

That's one I'd wanted to do too. I realize now that it was a sign that I might have left a hole in Lionel's training. I could tell him, but that wouldn't help him learn. And maybe I was too quick to tell him something rather than let him work it out. "Why do you think the spell doesn't already exist?"

"Because no one has found a way to get around the fact that it won't work if people believe what they are saying is the truth." He turned on the water and for a few minutes, all I heard was dishes being washed and rinsed. "I just thought I'd give it a try. But if you have any ideas, I'm open." I heard a drop of sulk in his voice, but he controlled it pretty well.

"I don't have any ideas. Anyway, the first part of the test is to work out what your spell should be. It's not just a matter of creating a spell. It's about creating the right one. There's nothing wrong with trying a truth spell, it's just very complex for your first attempt."

It would be really handy to have a truth spell right now. I didn't need The Morrigan to tell me not to trust everyone. If I could be confident in the truth, I would be able to make the right choices.

"Is it better to try a simple spell? Are there any left?"

"Good point. Why don't you think about a few options, and we can talk them through?"

"Maybe I can find a spell to keep Dionne from saying things she shouldn't." He laughed but I heard the possibilities in the words. "That might be more complicated than a truth spell."

He huffed a laugh. "I should probably figure out what I want to do when you don't need me any longer."

"Lionel, when you pass your test, you don't need to keep looking after me. I can hire someone or learn to be more self-sufficient." His spell wasn't one of my top priorities, and it should have been my only one, but once again, Lionel had to take a backseat. I swore I would find a way to make it up to him. I turned that thought into an oath as I waved down his objections. "So how do you think we should go about releasing Fionuir? If that's done, we'll have the druids off our case." And I would be one step closer to taking my life back.

"Are you sure you can send her to Maeve?"

As sure as I could be. I'd never put anyone in a dimensional fold before, so I was just playing a hunch. "Pretty sure. I will have to release her, and you'll have to keep a protection dome around us. The worst thing that could happen then is she'd show up in the circle."

"Do you want Dionne and Bud around? It could be a great lesson for both of them."

"I'm not sure enough of the release spell to put Dionne in the room, but Bud could come in handy as a witness if things go wrong." Would Dionne stay out of it? Maybe the fact she was at school would be a bonus. We could do the release when she wasn't around.

"Bud could be a messenger. We could contact the court through the circle downstairs, and she can confirm whether Fionuir has arrived."

I liked the idea of letting Bud show her skills as a go-between. Any way to combine things on the to-do list was welcome. "Maybe, and if she ever shows up in the morning as we agreed, we could get this done while Dionne is in school."

"You know, Quinn, I could do the release spell. If I used the charm you gave me, you could keep in contact with the court. That might be better. After all, the charm was created right after we imprisoned her. There's no chance we'd forget an aspect of the spell."

And if something went wrong, I would still be blind and unable to react fast enough. "No, you need to keep up the protections. I put her there, so it's my job to set her free. Besides, I didn't anticipate releasing Fionuir to a specific location when I made that charm."

Bud arrived mid-morning, an improvement of several hours on her past performance. We spent the afternoon in the workroom gathering the ingredients for the spell to release Fionuir.

"When will you know where to send her?" Bud was placing ingredients in order on the workbench. At least that's what she was supposed to be doing, and Lionel was tied up with his own tasks so he couldn't let me know if she was doing something wrong. "Will we visit the court again? That would be fun."

The wistful tone didn't fool me. She was hoping for another spying session. There was no guarantee she'd be as well behaved as the first time, and I was not going to facilitate the start of a battle of wits between the sidhe and the fairies. Both could be bloodthirsty enough to cause major problems for everyone. "We'll contact Maeve through the circle. Or, at least, we'll contact someone in her court." I realized I was making a major assumption that Maeve would agree to that type of communication.

"I should set the circle," Lionel said. "We could be done with this before Dionne comes."

I nodded in his direction, but kept my fingers moving across the ingredients. There were ten in all, and they were in the right order. It was a complex spell, but at least it was made with common ingredients. Rose petals, dried and powdery under my fingertips, but still pungent with the heavy scent of late summer. Cinnamon, bark rough against my skin; pepper, whole corns; honey boiled into a hard ball. Sage, lavender, rosemary, and parsley fresh cut from the garden; candle made from beef fat, and a fresh cut slice of ginger. "Bud, is the bowl clean?"

"Yes, Quinn Larson, and I have the fresh water in a jug. We are ready."

I heard Lionel muttering over the circle we needed in the center of the floor. "Let's hope that Maeve is ready for us." This was a time when I would have much preferred to be alone. It had to be perfect if it was going to work, and more people involved meant more opportunity for errors.

A feather touch of Bud's hand drew my attention.

"Quinn Larson, my mother is grateful that you saved her life. And so am I. If you hadn't, I wouldn't be here. I know that Fionuir stole your sight. Maybe we can convince her to give it back."

The kindness caught me off guard. I swallowed the lump in my throat before I answered. "She was very angry with me, Bud. I don't think that will have changed."

"No," Lionel said. "But we might be able to get that book back from her, the one with the spell to return your sight."

I hadn't forgotten that little fact, and I had been wondering how to get Maeve to give me the book when Fionuir was safely contained.

"Where is the book, Quinn Larson?"

"Fionuir has it in her pocket. It was there when I sent her away." I touched the ingredients again trying to take my mind off the book and put it back on the spell. "We'll ask Maeve when it's done. I don't want to complicate this any more than it already is." And I didn't want to get my hopes up either.

Bud and I waited outside the circle while Lionel tried to

contact Maeve through the link. I felt the change in air pressure as he sealed the circle.

"I can see what is happening, Quinn Larson. I thought circles were drawn to hide the magic."

"Usually they are opaque. I guess Lionel wants you to witness. Can you hear what's going on?" I couldn't make out any sound, but Bud would be able hear in a different range.

"No. I can only see Lionel. He is speaking. If I go closer, maybe I can hear?"

My heart dropped at the thought she would accidentally break the seal. I held up my hand. "No, just tell me what you see. Why don't you sit on my shoulder?" That way I'd know where she was.

She climbed my arm and sat before reporting, "He is placing something in the center. It looks like candy."

"That will be the price of using the link. There's a spirit in the court who will need to open the other end. Is the candy moving?"

"Yes, it is spinning around. Lionel is not speaking now. He looks scared. Oh, Quinn Larson, Lionel has fallen, and the candy is flying around." She grabbed my ear and squeezed.

This was not the expected reaction. "Bud, let go of my ear. What else can you see?"

I felt her stand on my shoulder. "It is hitting him. And bouncing off the circle. It looks like someone is trying to attack Lionel. Are you sure I shouldn't get closer?"

I shook my head. Accidentally breaking the circle could be fatal. "I mean, is there anyone else in the circle? A cloud? Or a light?"

"No, only Lionel. He is shouting."

Her weight shifted forward, and I reached up to hold her. She wiggled away from my hand. I was in no position to struggle with her for control.

"Nothing can get out, Bud, don't worry. Does Lionel look like he's asking for help?"

I struggled to keep my voice calm so she wouldn't panic. I

kept telling myself it was probably nothing. Lionel knew how to protect the circle. It was rare, but not unknown, for some spirit to come to the circle unbidden.

"No. He is shouting and now the candy is falling to the ground. Oh, there is a hole there. Now it is gone. Lionel is bleeding."

"Quinn, I am sorry. I don't know what happened." Lionel's voice came as though from a deep well as the circle dissipated. When it was gone his voice just sounded strained from the battle he had fought. "It's gone, but I'll have to cleanse the room again. Do we have time before Dionne gets here?"

"Bud says you're hurt." I sniffed the air for signs of whatever had invaded his spell.

"The candy winged me. It's just a scratch."

Bud tsked. "No, Lionel, it is bleeding. Let me fix it."

I waited until the fussing stopped before asking, "We have time as long as Maeve comes to the circle right away, but we can always do this after Dionne goes home." So much for getting this task off the list of things I had to do. "Who was it?"

Lionel shushed Bud's chatter. "Bud, please take the cloth and clean it. We don't want the blood to interfere with any other spells. I'll tell Quinn what happened while you're gone."

"Okay, but don't say anything interesting until I'm done."

"I will just tell him what you would have seen anyway, Bud."

I smiled. "Bud, don't pretend you won't be listening."

Lionel touched my shoulder before he settled beside me. I would miss his thoughtfulness when he left. Despite his assurance he would stay, he needed to go out into the world when he was finished his apprenticeship.

"I don't know who it was. I hadn't even called anyone. The spirit was waiting. I think it's gone, but what happens if it's waiting again?"

"It's not a disaster. You'll have to go to the court and make arrangements. We'll postpone the spell until it's safe to cast it. What exactly happened?"

"It is clean now, Quinn Larson. Lionel, drink this, it will make you feel better."

Lionel would have to check on Bud's cleaning ability. Fairies were fast, but that was too fast. Lionel thanked her and I heard him swallow what must have been water. At least they seemed to have put aside their squabbling.

"Thank you, Bud. The spirit, or whatever it was, just kept saying *no don't do it. It is too dangerous. Stop before it is too late.*"

Typical. "We'll that's pretty vague. No indication of what we are supposed to stop? Fionuir's release? Training Dionne? Something totally random?"

He sighed. "No. It's probably just a mad spirit. I'll check that there's no blood, and then we can try again."

"I cleaned the blood that got on the ground, Lionel." Bud was offended. I guess the truce between them was coming to an end.

Ignoring the pending argument, I focused on the intruder. "You said 'whatever it was'. What did you mean by that?"

"It felt... I don't know, empty is the best word to describe it. Maybe it's just a type of spirit I've never encountered." He drifted away, and I heard him quietly muttering a cleansing spell. Then he stopped part way through, his voice surprised, "Bud, how did you cleanse this so fast? Can you teach me?"

"No, it's a fairy secret. Can I help you with the circle?"

"No. It's a wizard secret. I'll call Maeve now." Then the silence descended as I assume he drew a circle.

Bud narrated and within five minutes, Lionel was finished with the spell.

"Maeve has a prison available. She asks you to send Fionuir to the center of the court. They'll deal with her. Maeve will keep the court empty for one hour."

"That should be enough. Let's get started."

12

J ust as Lionel finished preparing a new circle so we could release Fionuir, I heard footsteps approach the door to the workroom. "Quinn, I'm here. What's going on?"

"Wait a minute," I called back. "Lionel, what time is it? I thought we still had a couple of hours before Dionne got here."

"We do. Shall I go let her in?"

As much as I didn't want her to be here in case something went wrong, I couldn't think of a way to keep her upstairs long enough for us to finish. I nodded and waited until she joined us. "Aren't you supposed to be in school? I don't want you in trouble for playing hooky."

She laughed. "No one says hooky anymore, grandpa. I have a half day off. I promise I'm not skipping out."

"Call me grandpa again and you'll by reciting spell inventories for a month. We're releasing Fionuir. I need you to stay safely outside the circle with Bud."

"Why are we going to be out here?" Bud asked. "I can help, Quinn Larson. You know I can."

Before Dionne could add her two cents, I said, "I need you

out here in case something goes wrong. Dionne, you know how to contain a circle if need be, and Bud can go get help if you can't clear the room."

"Okay. I get to practice spells, that's cool." Dionne sounded like she wanted to argue but chose to look at the positive side instead.

I told myself that I'd need to let her do real magic at some point. I just wish we had more time before it became life or death. "This is important, Dionne. Lionel and I will be vulnerable. If there's a problem and you can't contain the circle, the damage will spread. Lionel and I can handle whatever happens inside. Don't break the circle no matter what you think you see." It sounded like I believed it.

"She can do it, Quinn," Lionel chimed in. "We were practicing small circles yesterday."

"I have every confidence," I lied. "Bud, how quickly can you get help? Not that I think we'll need it."

"I can go to the park and be back with help in a few minutes. I will have to make everyone sneak in because humans will be around. But it will be fast. I promise, Quinn Larson."

"Then you need to go as soon as there is a problem. Don't try to help Dionne, just go." There was nothing else for me to do. I held out my hand for Lionel to guide me to the center. "Make sure they can see through it."

"I know, Quinn. Please, just stand there and let me concentrate. I don't want a repeat of the last circle. That is what you're trying to protect against, right? Not a problem with Fionuir?"

I hadn't thought further than trying to make sure that we had a clean circle. I knew we'd send Fionuir to the sidhe court. "I don't like what's been happening lately in the circles. Ever since we tried to find out about Dionne's parents, I've felt like there's something waiting for us to make a mistake."

"Me to make one, you mean. Just like I did a few minutes ago."

Lionel shuffled around me as he spoke. "I am being as thorough as possible."

"I don't think you made a mistake, Lionel. I mean us. If you weren't capable of simple circle work, I wouldn't be preparing you to graduate." I couldn't help but think that the 'something' wasn't just waiting for us. It was starting to sap Lionel's confidence.

"Okay, the circle is ready."

I nodded and started picturing Fionuir the last time I saw her. That was days before I imprisoned her but would still be enough. I felt Lionel station himself at my back. We took turns tossing the ingredients at our feet and calling the power from them. I crumbled the rose petals last and felt the final layer of strength fill me. I was casting the spell through a dimension, and that was like trying to hit a target across the world. The power from the ingredients would add focus as well as strength.

"I call Fionuir from her prison to Maeve's court." The first call was quiet and respectful. The second call loud and angry. "I command Fionuir to Maeve for whatever actions are deemed necessary. I remove all claims I have upon her for justice or revenge for her acts against me."

I expected to feel a pressure release, but I didn't feel anything. Of course, I had never released a prisoner from a dimensional fold before. I'd never imprisoned anyone before either, and that had worked as expected. "Lionel, contact the court and see if Fionuir has arrived."

I heard him speak the spell to open the channel to Maeve. There was a pause that seemed to take forever and then a warm breath of cloves and incense.

Lionel asked the question and a warm female voice answered so quietly I couldn't make out the words.

"Thank you," Lionel said. The scents cut off abruptly.

"Well?"

"She didn't appear in the court. Do you think you sent her somewhere else?"

The breath left me at the thought of an angry Fionuir on the loose. "There must be a way to find her. Clear the circle, and we'll figure it out. We don't have much time either way."

We left the workroom and settled in the kitchen. What I wanted to do was slam my fist into the wall and swear a blue streak, but that wouldn't do more than feel really good as I did it. The aftermath of my temper tantrum was more likely that everyone would shut down. I needed them thinking and finding a solution.

"Can you tell if she's still in the prison?" Dionne's question came over the sound of water going into the kettle. If only there was a tea to help solve sidhe problems. "I mean, we need to know what we're dealing with. If she's free... Well, I don't know what might happen, but I've never seen you so worried."

"I hope you never find out." I closed my mouth before anything else could get out. With Lionel thinking he was making mistakes, I didn't want him to think I agreed. Even blind, I could see a red mist at the edge of my senses. I needed to take a mental breath and the only way to do that without snapping was to get the others talking. "Lionel, any ideas?"

"Yes, but I don't know if it will help."

"What is it?" A bit of my annoyance slipped through in my tone.

He coughed before answering. "I think you should go kick a wall or something. You look like murder."

"Yes, Quinn Larson." Bud's hand landed on my ear. "You are glaring at everything."

I shook my head. "We don't have time for me to indulge in emotions. We have to get this done, so we can deal with the prophecy."

"My counselor always tells me to deal with anger, so it doesn't fester," Dionne said. "We're all kind of pissed off, Quinn. But you look like you are about to have a stroke. If you don't want to express it in front of us, go somewhere and get it over with."

I opened my mouth to argue and realized the truth. We'd wasted time already by arguing. I was lucky to have such mature apprentices. I would try to remember that in the future. "Lionel, put a silence spell on my room. You can remove it when I come out."

I felt my way to my room and slammed the door behind me. Knowing I could do whatever I needed to didn't help. Anger wasn't supposed to be intellectual. It just felt like another thing on my to-do list, another thing to deal with.

I kicked at where I thought my bed was, hoping the action would trigger something. All I managed to do was tangle my foot in a pile of clothes.

I couldn't just go back out to the kitchen. The anger was still there, so I felt behind me for the wall and stomped my way around the room. Each step was accompanied by a different swear word for the first ten stomps. Then I repeated the series.

I'd forgotten how satisfying a good stomp could feel. By the second circuit of the room, I was laughing. At the end of the third circuit, the hysteria had drained from the sound. I was left with a chuckle and a clear head.

I closed my door behind me and told Lionel to clear the spell. "I have an idea. Go get the charm I gave you to release Fionuir in case I was gone."

"But you said you need to release her."

"I know, but if the charm still exists, Fionuir is still imprisoned. If she's free, the charm will be erased."

"Right. I'll be back in a second." I heard his steps bang across the room.

"If she's still there, we'll try again, and this time we'll all be inside the circle. Lionel can cast it wide enough."

"I thought it was too dangerous." Dionne handed me a mug of cool tea. "What's different?"

"Nothing might be different, but if the first spell doesn't work, we don't have time to clear and reset a circle. We have to keep trying until Maeve's time limit is over."

Lionel's door slammed. "It's still active, Quinn. Fionuir is still there."

13

I took the charm, a walnut, and tested the boundaries. "It looks like I set the trigger for you or me to use." I hadn't remembered that. What else had I forgotten?

Lionel touched my hand. "Let's just use the charm. It'll be faster, and we don't have much time before Bud and Dionne have to leave." He didn't say that we needed to get this done before another mad spirit got in our way.

"I don't know that it will work to put her in the court."

"We could contain her somehow if she came here. We could talk to Maeve about giving us more time. You and I can work through the night. Or do you think we need Bud and Dionne for some reason?"

Wondering the same thing, I examined the need I felt to have them in attendance. "I think we need witnesses, or back up. It doesn't have to be Dionne or Bud."

"We could call for Beacon, or Olan, if we have to." Lionel touched my elbow. "Let's get going."

I followed them down to the workroom. "That will take time, and I'm not comfortable bringing anyone else into this right now." The druids might see it as a violation of the deal.

We gathered in the center of the circle and waited while Lionel set the protective spells. I listened carefully as he used the moment to train Dionne. The spells were set perfectly and strengthened by the addition of a little of her power. She learned quickly – almost as if the knowledge was there and we just had to open the channels.

Lionel finally stopped giving instructions. "Right, it's done, Quinn. Are you ready?"

I took a breath. "Yes. If everyone can find a place to settle, I'll do it."

A murmur of agreement was broken when Dionne said, "Bud, settle. That means keep still."

"Yes, I know that. But I'm so excited it is hard to settle."

I sighed before I could stop myself. Apparently, I'd released my inner teenager along with the anger I'd shed. "Bud, when you are the leader of your tribe, you will have to have some patience. At least, you will have to have more than your followers."

"Yes, I understand, I am sorry. Now, I am settled, Quinn Larson." The apology didn't come through in her voice.

I took the walnut and rubbed it between my thumb and fourth finger. The spell wasn't difficult, just precise. The scent of almonds and vanilla rose as the first layers of the spell lifted.

I visualized the complexity of the spell as a series of leaves wrapped around the nut. After the scent came the sound of waves, and sand, and light breezes through ripe wheat. Then blackness pierced by a single point of light that I could see with my inner eye. That was the prison. My spirit rushed toward the light as though I was on an elastic and bouncing back to Fionuir. As I neared, I heard a scream. I felt anger boiling on the sound, its touch scoring my skin like fine whips.

If Fionuir were insane, we'd have a completely different set of problems.

I came to a stop. The pinprick of light hadn't grown, but I just knew that I was within touching distance of the prison. I called her name and the screaming stopped. The thick weight of her anger remained in the silence. "I am about to release you to the sidhe court." She couldn't answer, or at least I wouldn't hear if she answered. The scream had only been a manifestation of the emotion. Mere words didn't carry the power of fury.

"I will give you a moment to prepare." I had no idea if it would be painful, or frightening, or simply a change. The anger withdrew into the light. I touched the light and was drawn back to a chatter of voices.

"Wizard, you will regret your actions."

Fionuir was in the circle. I reached for power directly and started to chant a spell to hold her frozen.

"Bud, come back here," Dionne's voice made me stop my hand from releasing the spell.

"Everyone, get behind me," I screamed. I couldn't hold raw power much longer. There's a reason I use charms to contain spells, raw power is uncontrollable.

"Fool," Fionuir screamed.

"We're all clear," Lionel whispered in my ear.

I flung my power outward and heard a hiss that cut off abruptly.

"She's caught." Lionel grabbed my elbow. "Quinn, relax. I have you."

The world went silent, and I felt myself land in his arms.

I REGAINED CONSCIOUSNESS AND FELT SOMETHING TOUCHING my tongue. I was lying on the couch with a taste of sweetness in my mouth.

"See, I told you honey would work," Bud said.

Rubbing my eyes to drive away the confusion that lingered from the spell, I asked how long I'd been out.

"Only five minutes," Dionne said.

Lionel put a spoon in my hand and a bowl in my lap. "Fionuir is still downstairs. I put a containment circle in place, in case she found a way to get out of the spell you threw at her." He patted my hand. "Eat, you don't have much energy left, and we need you conscious."

I dug at the mixture and lifted a spoonful. Honey, dried fruit, nuts, energy food all right. I just didn't know how long the energy would last. "Is anyone hurt?" I should have asked that right away.

A squeak from near my head resolved itself into Bud's voice. "No, we're all fine, Quinn Larson. I think that—"

"I think you should go home, Bud. Enough excitement for one day. We'll see you in the morning." I was glad they were fine, but now with a mad sidhe in the workroom, it was time to make sure they stayed that way.

"But—"

"No. Both you and Dionne need to go. We're fine. The sidhe will come for Fionuir, and I'll sleep." I doubted that I would get any rest until she was safely in Maeve's control.

"Fine, Quinn Larson, I will see you tomorrow." Bud was going to have to learn she couldn't always do as she pleased, but I didn't have the strength to teach her today.

"You look like you need to rest for a week," Dionne said. "Lionel, make sure he doesn't stay up too long waiting for Fionuir to be picked up." She patted my shoulder and then called Bud to join her.

As soon as the door closed, I started the questions. "What exactly happened?"

"Fionuir snapped into the circle a second before you did. Other than the fact she was spitting fury, she didn't look harmed."

"That can't hurt in the long run. Maybe she'll calm down and get over it, maybe this millennium."

"I'm not sure we're that lucky. Anyway, you contained her before she did any damage, despite Bud flying around. Or maybe she distracted Fionuir long enough for you to act. It's hard to know with Bud whether she's extraordinarily lucky or has a real plan."

"I hope we're training her to rely more on the plan and less on the luck. Although I hear some humans think that fairies are the ones who bring luck."

"That wouldn't be a good thing. Not all of them are as... I don't know, normal seems wrong. Not all of them are less crazy than Princess and Bud."

I laughed. "Not all of them have the benefit of wizardly help."

"True, Quinn. Maybe you're a good influence."

Those words made me feel old. "We'll see. Look, I think Fionuir will stay frozen for about an hour. I won't have the energy to cast another spell strong enough to contain her by then. Can you call Maeve to come get her? Or is the containment circle taking all the room?"

"There's space for another small circle. I can contact Maeve," Lionel said. "Let's hope she can pick up her rival before anything else goes wrong."

I sat up. "Go ahead and make the call. I'll start some tea. We can celebrate one task being completed."

"What about the druids?"

I didn't want to think about them yet. "If they come, tell them what happened and ask them to come back later." I could hope it would work.

"Maybe they won't come. After all, if they were right, the souls will be at rest again, and they're not likely to come to you to make good on their end of the deal."

"We'll figure that out tomorrow. Go let Maeve know what happened."

FIFTEEN MINUTES AFTER LIONEL CONTACTED MAEVE, HE WAS opening the door to let in four sidhe men. I heard him give specific instructions as to where they had access.

"Quinn Larson," Owen, or Garnet, said. The twins were back in favor, or perhaps picking up the queen they had lost was part of their punishment. "Maeve sends her thanks."

"Tell her she's welcome. Now, please, do what you came to do." I pointed to the door to the workshop.

"Too bad you were not able to send Fionuir directly home. I am not surprised. You are not the wizard everyone thinks you are."

A pissing contest, just what I needed. "Not everything always goes to plan. I'm sure you realize that. After all, I seem to remember your plan to release her didn't go the way you wanted."

"Interfering wizards are a curse on any plans." Owen, or Garnet, I tried to think of them as separate rather than Owneor-Garnet, but it was hard. Whoever it was, their tone matched Fionuir's ferocity.

"At least I was able to release Fionuir. Perhaps it will mean something to her that you tried." I wasn't letting him off the hook. If he didn't want to fight with me, he could join his companions in the basement. "Is she likely to give you a reward for making the effort?"

"As I said, interfering wizards. I am sure you will come to regret your actions. Whether she will value our efforts or not, she will still wish you dead for imprisoning her."

Since the elections only ran every fifty years, I was pretty safe for the next forty-nine years as long as I kept on Maeve's good side. She would keep Fionuir under control – at least I hoped so. I wasn't naive enough to think Fionuir wouldn't try to get the throne back as soon as she could.

"Perhaps you are right. Now, I hear your companions returning. It would probably be a good idea to get Fionuir to the court before she recovers from containment. I don't think Maeve will be happy if you lose your prisoner. Or anyone is damaged in the journey."

The sound of voices grew louder, and then I felt more people fill the room. "Owen, take her arm and let us be going. I do not wish to delay until the humans fill the streets." Garnet sounded strained.

I couldn't bring myself to care about them being seen by humans. Even if they didn't have an adequate glamour to do what they needed, sidhe looked almost human, unnaturally beautiful humans, but close enough to pass. "If Maeve needs to contact me, she can call through a circle. Lionel will be monitoring."

I would be sleeping.

❧ 14 ❧

Another peaceful morning and it felt good to have one item on the accomplished side of the ledger. I was in the garden trying to figure out how to identify plants from feel. The aromatics were easy, I didn't need my fingers for those, but some of the more powerful plants didn't have a distinctive scent – and a few others had weapons that were best avoided.

I heard a rustle in the hydrangeas and tensed. Maeve would not have let Fionuir free, would she? I slipped a hand into my pocket to feel for defensive charms. I could get away with some overt magic since my neighbors were all asleep this early.

"Relax, Quinn Larson," Princess' voice was weak. "I have brought my irresponsible child to tell you something."

I blew out a breath and sat on the end of the garden bench. "It is good to hear your voice, Princess. You sound well."

"You flatter me, wizard. I am old and unattractive." The words didn't match her tone. On death's door or not, Princess had enough vanity to enjoy a compliment.

"What has Bud done?"

"She will tell you herself. I will rest here." She touched my knee as she spoke. "Do you have any honey?"

"Bud, wait a minute." I went to get a couple of spoonfuls of honey. While I was gone, I wondered what Bud could have done. Her apprentice oath would have taken care of anything that could hurt us. And she'd only been out of my sight – so to speak – for a few hours.

I held out the spoons when I got back, trusting that Princess wouldn't let them drop. "You might as well just tell me, Bud."

"Well, Quinn Larson, I don't really know why my mother is so angry. Do you think she might be ill? She is very old for a fairy."

"Daughter, do not make this worse. I might be old, but I can still make sure you are punished. You are not the leader of the Rose tribe yet."

"But it is a good thing I have done."

"I did not say it was a bad thing. It is not the thing you did. It is how you did this thing that is the problem."

I sat back and waited. Getting between bickering fairies was bad enough, but when they were mother and daughter, it could be deadly.

"But you said I might not be welcome back in Quinn's home." Bud's voice was laced with tears. I couldn't tell if they were real, or just for effect.

"That is up to Quinn Larson. You must tell him. Perhaps he will be happy." Princess patted my knee again. "Don't worry, Quinn. She will tell you. Please listen before you say anything."

There were a few sighs and false starts, but Bud finally crawled onto my lap. "Quinn Larson, I know that you wanted us to stay safe when you brought Fionuir out of her prison." She paused as if to let me say everything was all right, but I kept silent. "Well, Dionne and me were worried when she showed up. You couldn't see her face. She was very angry."

"What happened? I promise to listen." I ignored the acid churning in my stomach. Fionuir hadn't hurt anyone, so whatever Bud had done, it was forgivable – probably.

"I was very careful."

"Daughter! If I have to tell him, you will regret your cowardice." That was the voice of a leader.

"I will tell him, Mother. Just let me do it my way." The voice of the new leader.

If I wasn't afraid of what was coming, I would be fascinated at the change of the guard happening before me. "Ladies, let's start again. Bud, what did you do? Just tell me, and we'll deal with it."

It all came out in a rush. "When Fionuir appeared, I flew at her and stole something."

That could be a problem. Fionuir would have the right to retrieve her property. But perhaps we had some time to make it right. "Where is it? We can send Lionel to the court to return it."

"You might want to keep it for a while, Quinn," Princess said. "Bud, give it to him."

Bud hopped off my lap, and then I heard a series of clicks, like beads bumping together. "Hold out your hand." I obeyed and felt a book hit my palm. "It is the book of spells. The one that might help you get your sight back."

I tightened my fingers. "Thank you, Bud. You have done a good thing. We will have a little time before we needed to give it back. I guess we need Lionel. Bud, please go find him. Knock on his door, he may not be happy to have you burst into his room." I was able to keep the excitement from my voice – just barely. Bud did need to know that she'd taken a big risk, but this book was my freedom – and Lionel's.

A gentle cough brought my attention back to Princess. "Then I will go home. I trust you will punish my daughter appropriately?"

I swallowed the emotions in my throat. "If the apprentice oath doesn't stop her action, I'm not sure any punishment I can mete out will help."

"Quinn, the oath doesn't cover everything. Find a way to teach her to think before she acts. You've done wonders so far. I'm sure you'll find some way to deal with it."

Her confidence was energizing. "I'm beginning to think that the oath doesn't work the way I thought. Women seem to find a lot of loopholes."

She laughed. "Not women, Quinn Larson. You just don't notice when Lionel does things against your wishes. Now, I need to rest. I will speak to you in a few days. Good luck with the spell."

I thanked her and went back to the house to the sound of Lionel's exasperated protests.

I fell back on an old punishment, thanking whatever ruled the universe that cleaning always needed to be done. Bud was cleaning the kitchen in the human way, no magic, no flying. She'd grumbled a little, but I sensed her relief that I hadn't sent her home.

Lionel and I were sitting with the spell book between us. I kept my hands on the table while Lionel turned the pages.

"It's still not clear," he said. "We'll have to unlock the spell. I don't remember what page we found it on."

The book was only about four inches by three and fit into my palm easily. It weighed more than its size, which meant that its real dimensions were much larger. "It's okay. The spell might even move through the book. How many spider webs do we have in stock?" The last time we had this book, we'd discovered that the key to revealing the spells was an overlay of a spider web. And we'd found the spell just before Fionuir had attacked.

While I waited for Lionel to return, knowing we only had two or three webs, I started to think through a plan. Maeve wouldn't want to let me keep the book for long. If Fionuir had been able to speak, she'd have started demanding it right away. So, I thought we had a day or two at best. I was inclined to deal with this in a day anyway. The impatience for my sight was threatening to override my common sense.

"Four," Lionel announced.

A screech came from the kitchen.

I pushed away from the table. "Bud, what's wrong?"

"Nothing is wrong, Quinn. I was singing. It helps to pass the time."

I settled back in the chair and gritted my teeth. "Are you almost finished?"

"Yes, is there anything I can do to help? I can read spells; maybe I can find what you need."

I heard Lionel groan and gave him a stern look. "We'll let you know."

She returned to singing and I winced. Fairies had the weirdest taste in music. "So, four. The last time we found it was through sheer luck. How lucky are you feeling?" I asked.

"Not very, but maybe you can send Bud to get more webs anyway. Preferably somewhere we won't be able to hear her."

I wasn't feeling the universe aligning for me either, but we had to find the spell fast. "We'll do what we did last time. If Bud has to find more webs, then that's what will happen."

"You need spider webs? How many?" Bud settled her elbows on my lap. She was almost full grown now. The elbows were sharp, but she didn't weigh enough to make it painful.

"Let's try to find the spell." I closed my eyes. Four webs; it wouldn't take her long to replace them, but it would be better to do it later when the spiders were satiated and slow. "Bud, you pick the first page."

Lionel grunted his disapproval and started flipping the pages. "Tell me when to stop."

"Now, Lionel."

"Okay, hold the page flat, Quinn. When we found the spell last time you were touching the book. Maybe that will make the difference."

I took the book and flattened the page. A moment later, I felt the sticky brush of the web. No one spoke. "Well?"

"Don't move. It's not the spell we need, but it's one for

slowing time. Let me get some paper. We might as well record what we find."

He had a point, and I remembered the greed for new spells. I realized that I hadn't felt it since Cate died. I hadn't noticed the lack of curiosity, perhaps it was part of the grieving process.

"Okay," Lionel said after scribbling the spell instructions. "Who guesses next? I think it should be you, Quinn. It's your spell that we're looking for after all."

I didn't want to guess. I didn't know if I could take the disappointment if I guessed wrong. "You go next, Lionel. I'll take the last two webs if we need them"

"Okay, if you are sure." He took the book back and I heard rifling paper. "This one."

He passed me the book, and I held it flat; my heart beating fast with hope that I couldn't quite suppress.

"Not what we're looking for, but it's a spell to place a life force into an object. That's gross. Let me write it down anyway."

I wondered why Fionuir would need that spell. "What does it require?"

"Quinn Larson, do you need to capture someone?" Bud asked.

I didn't think so, but you never know. "I was thinking we could reverse it. If we could release something, it would be good."

"Like the spirits in the amulet? That might make the druids angry, Quinn Larson."

She was right, but I still didn't want to pass up a powerful spell. "Lionel, do you have it?"

"Yes, it's pretty easy, considering. I've written it down and drafted a reversal. You can check it when you have your sight back."

I liked his confidence. "Okay, we've got two more. Flip the pages and I'll pick." If we found the spell we needed, I would send Bud out for more webs, and we'd get as many spells as possible before we returned the book.

I found a spell to create a wall from air.

"One more then Bud will need to go web gathering," Lionel said.

"I will gather as many as you need. I will only find the best webs. I noticed there were seven spiders in your garden, Quinn Larson. Perhaps we can get enough webs for each page in the book. Should I start now?" Her excitement pushed her voice high enough that I had difficulty hearing the last words.

"We'll start with a few, Bud. I'm not sure we need to get all the spells out of Fionuir's book. I'll settle for just the right one."

Lionel took the book from me. "So, should we do the last web now?"

Torn between wanting to get the whole thing over with, and fearing we would never find the right spell, I said, "Let's do it. Then we'll have lunch. Unless I'm completely wrong, we need food more than we need new spells."

"I am hungry, Quinn Larson, but I will wait so I can find you webs first."

I was touched. Fairies burned calories too fast to miss a meal. "No. Lunch first, no matter what we find with this web." I nodded to Lionel to start flipping pages. Then reached out and placed my finger in the book to stop the noise. "Place the web."

I waited and then heard a sigh.

"Sorry, Quinn, it's just a spell for a glamour. We have plenty of them."

A good teacher doesn't take out his emotions on his students. I don't know where I heard that, but I took it as a rule. I gently closed the book. "That's okay. We have two new spells, and we'll keep trying."

15

I hated taking webs from spiders for nothing. It felt like I was taking food directly from their mouths. So, we had Bud go out and collect three webs at a time, promising each other that we would stop when we found the spell that would restore my sight. Even so, we spent the afternoon finding spells and using more webs. Lionel remembered to mark the pages we'd already tried, which at least made me feel like we were being efficient.

On her fourth trip, Bud flew back to the room talking all the way from the door. "There's an old human. He is too near for me to hide from. Quinn Larson, I cannot collect more webs until he is gone. I am sorry, Quinn Larson. I cannot go back." She took a deep breath.

I didn't know whether to laugh or slam my fist into the nearest wall in frustration. We were so close to getting my sight back I could almost feel the joy of being able to watch the sun set, but every sound made me think there was a sidhe at the door to demand the book back, and it wouldn't be long before the fear became reality. "Relax, Bud. We can take a break. Do you have any webs with you?"

"Thank you, Quinn Larson. Yes, I have two. Are we going to use them now?"

I pressed the pages of the book between my hands. Would a short break help? Could I manage to wait? "Lionel, what do you think? You've written out ten new spells, should we do two more then wait until my neighbor is finished in his garden?"

"It doesn't seem right to delay. Actually, Dionne will be here soon. We'll have another hand to write spells and she can gather webs unquestioned. I would love to continue collecting spells even when we find the one we need." He took the book from me. "I know, let's try this. We'll use the two webs. Then take a break. If the old man is still there, I can teach Dionne how to harvest webs. Or I can try, but you know I'll lose half of them before we can use them."

He knew his limitations, and he knew when to let someone else do the work. He would make a great teacher.

"Okay, give me the book." I ran my fingers across the cover trying to feel something to give me direction, but there was nothing. I opened the book and started flipping pages. "Bud, do you have a lucky number?"

"Yes, Quinn Larson, it is four hundred and eighty-two."

"That's a good number, but I don't think there are that many pages. Lionel?"

"Sixteen, but if we are going to use that system, shouldn't we use yours?"

"I want to test an idea." I closed the book and then flipped to page sixteen. "What spell would you want this to be? Not the one to give me back my sight – that's my spell."

He tapped his fingers on the table. I was surprised that he had to think about it. After a few seconds, he said, "A spell to preserve a life. Not to save it, but to protect the person from harm."

"That's a long shot. Put the web in place, Bud." I held my breath and tried not to get my hopes up.

"Quinn Larson! It worked."

My heart stopped and the world went cold. I took a deep breath and asked, "What spell is it?"

"Um, well," Lionel's dithering almost had me snapping at him. "It's a spell to place a shell around someone. It has to be someone who won't move, but still it would protect them."

I heard pen scratching. "Let me know when you are done."

It took a few minutes. Time I could barely manage to live through. "Okay, so what's your lucky number?"

"Forty." I snapped the book closed and started turning pages. When I got to forty, I couldn't speak. Fortunately, no one needed my instruction. I felt the whisper of spider silk against my fingers. And then I waited and waited. Finally, I had to ask, "What is it? Just tell me."

"It's not for your eyesight. It's called a stolen moment spell."

I'd never heard of it. "Can you understand what it's supposed to do?" Maybe it would give a moment of sight. Better than nothing.

"As far as I can tell it allows you to create a moment with a missing loved one," Lionel said. "I'll write it down while you figure out what to do next."

Bud patted my shoulder. "I know you will figure it out, Quinn Larson. I won't let the sidhe take the book until you find the spell."

I tried to borrow some of her confidence. I was so sure that the spell would be there.

"Hey, guys, what are you doing?" Dionne dropped something heavy before sitting at the table.

"We are trying to find a spell to cure Quinn Larson's blindness." Bud explained what we had done so far. "Now we need some more webs and an idea."

"Do I have to get webs?"

I pulled myself back to the conversation. "Check to see if any of the neighbors is in their yard. If it's clear, Bud will collect some more webs. If not, Lionel can show you what to do."

"Okay, I'll check." She clomped to the back window. "No. There's no one in sight." The relief was evident in her voice.

"I will bring five webs, because that is all I can carry."

"Be careful, Bud. We have time." I took the book back from Lionel. "I don't really have an explanation for what just happened. I had no desire for the new spell."

"I have an idea," Dionne said. "I think you get the thing you really want this way, whether you know it or not. Like, Lionel wants to keep people safe."

"That's not true. I want to be a full wizard. And to study."

"And to make sure no one gets hurt. Like Cate was hurt. Let me finish. I know Quinn wants to get his sight back, but I think he wants to bring Cate back more. He knows he can't really bring her back from the dead. Recreating moments would be the next best thing." Her voice caught on the last words.

"Dionne, you can't cast that spell without my direct permission."

"I know," she snapped. "Oh, god. I'm sorry, Quinn. I know it's probably dangerous and everything. But it's a spell to bring back a person."

"It might not be." I didn't believe we could bring people back, at least as anything other than a spirit. "It might just bring something back from your memory."

"Sure." I heard the disappointment she was trying to hide. "Anyway, we should keep working on this."

I wanted to keep her thinking about spells rather than her parents. "So, do you have an idea how to find the spell without going page by page?"

I heard Dionne flipping through the book. "You found it once. You can find it again. There are only about a hundred pages in the book. Even if we go page by page it won't take too long."

"It's not that simple. We won't be able to get that many webs before the spiders revolt." And we didn't have enough time to write out each spell before the sidhe would be here.

"Okay, what did you and Lionel do last time?"

Lionel answered, "I just kind of knew where the spell was. Well, the first one. There are two."

"And we've tried to recreate that," I said. "It didn't work." I filled in the rest of the details.

"Okay, let me think for a minute." After a few minutes that felt like an eternity, Dionne said, "Has Bud looked for a spell?"

"Not yet. Why?" I was starting to feel hope that Dionne would come up with a different angle.

"What if you only get lucky once? That if you want the spell to be there, the book will open to that page. But only one time."

"I have five webs!" Bud announced in a rush. "But I think we need to leave the hunt for a day. The spiders were coming to stop me."

"Good work, Bud. That should be enough. We can spend the evening learning the spells we found, if this doesn't work. We won't be allowed to keep the book much longer."

Bud tapped my knee. "I told you that I would stop them taking the book. Did you find out what to do?"

"Dionne has an idea," Lionel said.

"Well, it won't get any better with waiting," Dionne said. "Give me the book. I'll try, and if it works, Bud can find the second spell."

I pushed myself up from the table. "I can't just sit here and wait. I'll make tea."

"It will only take a minute, Quinn," Dionne said.

"I'll fill the kettle then."

The silence was heavy with hope. As the water poured into the kettle, I imagined that Dionne was feeling her way through the pages, looking for a clue, something that would guide her.

"Okay, here, drop the web here. And don't touch me with it. Oh gross!"

So much for reverence. "Well?"

"Just a second, Quinn, it's not the spell I saw, but I think... yes. It's the other spell. That's good, right?"

My knees went weak. "Yes, that's good."

"Let me find the other spell now," Bud said, her voice suddenly solemn. "It will make everyone happy to have Quinn seeing again."

I felt my way back to the table, all my practice at finding my way around suddenly gone. "Thank you, Bud. Let's get this done. I don't think I can take much more of a delay."

"Bud, get up on the chair," Dionne said. "It will be easier for you to hold the book on the table."

"Yes, it's a good idea. So, I just turn the pages until I decide that the spell we need is on one?"

"That's what I did. Then Lionel will put on the web."

The screeching started again. "Bud, do you have to sing?"

"It is my way of calling the spell to me, Quinn Larson." She started again.

After a few choruses, she said, "Here, this page."

I knew Lionel was working as fast as he could, and that webs were delicate, but I just needed to hear the words, one way, or another.

"It's the right one," Lionel breathed the words.

16

His words didn't register for a moment. As much as I wanted it to be the right page, part of me didn't believe I would ever get my sight back.

"It's not that complicated to do, I think we have most of the ingredients," Lionel said. "We have a few more webs; can I use them up? Uh, Quinn, are you okay?"

My "yes" came out as a croak. I cleared my throat and started again. "Yes, I'm fine. Go ahead and use the webs. It would be a waste not to. Let me know when you are done."

I returned to the boiling kettle. Now that we were close to it, I started to worry. What if the spell didn't work? What if it only partially worked? Measuring the tea into the pot, I told myself to let it go. If the spell didn't work, I was no worse off. I'd just have to accept my blindness. If it didn't completely work, how would that be worse?

"Let me help you, Quinn Larson." Bud startled me. "I will carry the mugs and you can bring the tea... and some more honey?"

"Sorry, Bud, we should have eaten again a long time ago. I'll bring the honey jar, and you can help yourself."

"Really? I've never had a whole jar." The mugs in her hand clinked together enough to tell me she was dancing around.

"You probably shouldn't eat the whole jar." I didn't want Princess coming around chastising me for putting Bud into a sugar coma. "Thank you for helping."

"It was my pleasure. Sometimes a leader must face the thing that she fears. Now that I've faced the displeasure of spiders, who knows, maybe I will be able to face humans."

"Let's not get ahead of ourselves."

Lionel took the pot from me. "Okay, Quinn, we've got the spell and three more; a soft glow spell, a time stopping one, and a new summoning spell. Maybe we should eat too. Bud's not the only one who missed a meal."

"I'm not sure I can wait until you've cooked dinner. Can we just go through the ingredients first?"

"Lionel looks like he's about to pass out, Quinn," Dionne said. "Look, I can read his writing. Go make toast or something, Lionel."

I felt a pit in my stomach. "You're right. If we are going to do the spells, we shouldn't be hungry."

"Okay there are a bunch of ingredients I recognize from my lessons, and a few I don't. The first spell is a paste we make to cover your eyes. The second one is the cleanser for the paste. You wear the paste for two hours, and when you clean it off, your eyesight should return. Oh, we need to figure out how to explain your sudden cure to Ms. Metcalfe."

I'd forgotten the social worker. "We'll think of something," I said. I wasn't sure if I was confident or didn't care. "Read the spells please, Dionne."

"Okay, mix blood from an eagle with dirt that has covered a hidden grave. Add sage smoke and mix with fairy tears. Take sap from the deepest root of the oldest tree within walking distance, and blend with the mixture. Call the spirits to the spell and paint over the eyes of the victim. Wait exactly two hours and remove."

I had most of the ingredients, and others were easy enough to get. The sap was going to be a problem. "Does it say that we need to use the second spell to remove it?"

"Yes. It's pretty easy," Lionel answered. "Here, toast with cheese."

I took a bite and suddenly realized how hungry I felt. "Perfect, thanks. Dionne, can you read the second spell?"

"You need ground acorns, obsidian, mallow furze, some clean muslin, and rainwater from a storm on the full moon. You cut the muslin with the obsidian, so I guess that's a knife. Then you mix the acorns and mallow furze with the water and use it to wash away the paste."

I finished my toast while I tried to figure out how long it would take to find the missing ingredients.

"Oh, yeah, we have to call a different set of powers. I can do the mixing, and Lionel can call the powers. We could do it right now." Dionne's chair scraped the floor.

I waved at her to sit. "There are a few ingredients I don't have."

She sighed. "I guess there isn't an ingredient store, right?"

Lionel laughed. "No, but that would be a great idea."

"Magic isn't supposed to be that easy," I said. "I think we have everything on the second list. Lionel? You have been gathering ingredients lately. Am I right?"

"Yes, I gathered the rain last week, because we always need it. And we have eagle blood and plenty of sage in the garden."

"Dirt from a hidden grave, fairy tears, and the sap," Dionne said.

"I will get you all the fairy tears you need, Quinn Larson. I will need something to carry them in. If I eat all the honey, this jar would be a good vessel."

"Thank you, Bud. I'm sure Lionel can find you something easier to carry." I dreaded the thought of the grave dirt.

"The sap? Could Beacon get it for us?" Dionne asked.

There were still so many gaps in her education. "I don't think Moss will let him draw sap. It's kind of the opposite of what sprites do."

"So how are you going to get it? If it can't be drawn from the tree."

"The druids might have some," Lionel said. "They use all kinds of things like sap in their rites. I could ask them."

"It can't hurt to ask. Don't agree to anything unless I'm there. The price might not be worth getting my sight back." The druids were quite capable of demanding a blood sacrifice, or worse.

"That leaves the dirt," Dionne said. "Where would we find a hidden grave?"

I swallowed the grief that flooded me as I tried to answer. "I buried Cate in the back yard. Only a few people know about it."

"I can get that too," Lionel said.

I held up my hand. This was my responsibility. "I will dig it out, Lionel."

"She wouldn't hold it against you, Quinn. It wasn't your fault she died." Lionel's voice caught on the last words. "I mean it wasn't really anyone's fault."

"We'll go when it's dark," I said. "You can talk to the druids right after. Who knows? We might be doing the spell tomorrow evening." I couldn't deny Dionne the chance to participate in the spells, one more day wouldn't make a difference.

The oak tree was in the back of the garden. I hadn't been near it since the night I buried Cate. No matter how much I thought I was through the grieving, no matter that I had forgiven Dionne for accidentally summoning the demon that took Cate's life, pain tore my heart when I even thought of going into that corner. It was easy to pretend it wasn't there while I was blind. I didn't know how it would feel when I could see her grave. Would I be able to enjoy my garden again?

"Are you sure I can't do this for you, Quinn."

"No. I'll do it. I need to it. Give me the bag and trowel." I kept my voice calm. "Could you leave me alone?"

"I'll wait on the porch," he whispered.

The trowel in my right hand and the bag clutched in my left, I felt my way to the tree. I'd buried her close, but there was no mound, no indication that someone lay under the overgrown grass.

There were tears burning my eyes as I arrived at the grave. There was no doubt in my mind where I was. The memory of burying her flooded my mind. I staggered with the weight of pain that surged through me. I should be past this by now. I should be healed.

I lowered myself to the ground and touched the earth. I could sense the seam where I'd replaced the turf, but all there was beneath the sod was dirt. Cate was long gone. The grave wasn't apparent to the casual glance, but I felt the scar through the tangled roots – a scar that was echoed somewhere inside me.

I took a deep breath and tried to regain my equilibrium. I had gotten past this point. I would be fine. Cate would want me to get my sight back. She would be putting the soil in the bag herself if she could.

I used the trowel to slice the top of the sod from the soil, and then I dug out a small amount of earth to place in the bag. Testing it with my fingers, about a half cup, I realized we'd need to dry it out to make it work. I placed the sod back into place and whispered a charm to heal the damage, and another goodbye to Cate. I closed my eyes and felt some of the pain I carried slip into the earth.

I walked back to the house and handed Lionel the bag. "It's time to go find the druids. I need to get back to training you and Dionne."

While Lionel was gone, I did something I should have done a long time ago. I thought about Cate. The emotions that tore me apart in the garden were a complete surprise. I thought I had dealt with her death, but I guess I'd just pushed it away. If I didn't let the emotions out, I knew I would regret it, and one day it would taint my magic.

I was surrounded by potential irritants, and what chilled me was the thought that I was only holding my temper because I needed everyone to help me. For a wizard, being blind wasn't good in any circumstances, but if I was alone, I wouldn't be able to do magic. I would just survive from day to day. I couldn't afford to hold this in any longer.

When I had my sight back, I might not find the reserves of patience I needed. I might... well, I might lash out at Dionne. She didn't deserve that, even if she wasn't one of the prophesied.

I fumbled for a candle and match and then carefully lit the wick. It was simple to place the candle in front of me. The heat from the flame was enough to tell me where it was located. I took a pinch of the dirt that Lionel had spread on a plate to dry. Holding my hand above the flame, I started the ritual.

"I'm sorry that I didn't protect you," I whispered and sprinkled a few grains of dirt into the flame. I heard hissing and smelled the mossy aroma of burning dirt.

"I'm sorry I didn't tell you sooner that I loved you." Sprinkle of dirt.

"I'm sorry I don't miss you more."

"I'm sorry I am still alive."

The dirt was gone from my fingers. I took another pinch and began the second half of the ritual.

"I am glad I knew you." Dirt into the flame. This time the aroma was tinged with lemon and lavender, proving that the spell was working.

"I am glad for my memory of the kiss we shared."

"I am glad you knew I loved you at the end."

"I am glad to be alive to protect others."

With the last words, I felt something inside break. Tears were racing down my cheeks. I leaned over the heat of the candle, letting them fall into the wick and douse it.

When the tears stopped, I felt new, and empty. Warmth flowed into me on a sound of laughter and joy. I hurt, but it was starting to heal.

❧ 17 ❧

I woke later when Lionel returned.

"Quinn, I am sorry it took so long, the druids were meeting when I arrived, and they made me wait. Myrddin is here and has the sap, but he needs to talk to you before he can hand it over."

I hadn't heard Lionel enter, so I had no idea that Myrddin was with him. I gestured to the chair. "Say what you need to, Myrddin. It has been a long day."

"Wizard Larson, we are willing to provide you with the sap we have held for many decades, but there is a price." His voice was a whisper that had an edge. Something that would bother him that much was going to be a problem for me.

"I did not imagine you would be willing to give the sap to me without cost. Did Lionel tell you what I need it for?"

"He did, and we sympathize with your plight. Magic is a fickle thing. You must fear every spell you cast without your sight."

The words were meant to undermine my confidence. Why would he do that if he needed something? Although my confidence was untested since I hadn't cast much magic since Fionuir's spell handicapped me. "Care and fear are two different things,

Myrddin. I am sure the druids have learned that lesson over the millennia."

A dry rasp, that might have been a laugh, came from the druid. "It is a lesson all beings must learn, magic or not. But then, a wizard is always at the mercy of his certainty, delusional, or not."

I felt Lionel hovering. "Perhaps you can make some refreshments, Lionel. Myrddin, would tea be acceptable?" I hoped he would say he was too busy. I needed to sleep, a side effect of the grieving ritual, and I needed to know what the bargain was, and his attitude was getting on my nerves.

"I need nothing. Let us get down to business. The souls in the amulet are still restless."

"I released Fionuir, our bargain is complete."

"No one is disputing that, wizard. It seems that the coming of the prophecy of the six is disturbing their world."

That was interesting. I thought the emergence of the fifth being was a secret. Then again, the druids were the holders of secrets. "So, the prophecy is going to come to be? Were the souls restless the last time we came this close?"

"That is not information you need to do what we ask as the price for curing your sight. It seems that this time the course is set for the prophecy, but nothing is certain until it happens. And that brings us to the bargain. When you stop the prophecy, we will provide you with the sap."

I suppressed my first reaction; it would have been stupid to let out my surprise. I was careful not to say anything that could be construed as acceptance. "Do you know how I can accomplish that? After all, no one seems to know much about the prophecy. And we only know that the six are emerging, not who they are." If the druids knew Dionne was one of the six, they wouldn't be asking me to stop the prophecy. She would already be dead, or worse. "And I am blind."

"I have no information for you. We do not care what methods you use. We only wish to have the souls find peace again."

"If you were wrong about Fionuir, what makes you confident that the prophecy is the cause?" There was no way I was going to mess with the prophecy, but maybe Myrddin would let something slip, and we'd get a little closer to understanding what was going on.

"We are confident. That is all you need to know. We do not believe it is necessary for the prophecy to come to be in any particular time. We have sought for the lines of consequence and cannot see anything in the future that is desirable if the six should fulfill their destiny."

Not desirable for druids maybe, but that didn't mean it would be bad for anyone else. "If I were to agree, I am not agreeing you understand?" I waited for a noise indicating that he understood. "If I were to agree, how would you advise me to proceed?"

"There are certain ceremonies we can conduct to gather together the scraps of information about the prophecy. We would do so and provide you with whatever information came to us."

"And if it does not calm the souls? If I am successful and the prophecy does not happen, what if they are still restless?"

"If you bring an end to the prophecy of the six, we will honor the bargain."

I didn't miss the fact that they had switched their focus. It was all about the prophecy. Had they already asked others to do this?

"Quinn," Lionel said. "I only know of one way to stop, or at least delay, the prophecy."

I reached out to him and squeezed his arm. If he slipped now and let the druids know about Dionne, it would be a disaster.

"Myrddin, if you can gather the information, why do you need me? Why can't you act on it?"

He cleared his throat, and I congratulated myself on discomfiting a druid. It was not an easy feat. "We do not have unlimited energy. We have learned that you are our best hope to stop the prophecy, but we were unable to discern the reason. The ceremonies needed to stop it ourselves will drain us of our strength for too long. We cannot allow anything to distract us from protecting the contents of the museum. The last time we attempted it, Fionuir was able to take the amulet."

"I can see why you want to avoid that happening again," I said. "You know I think if I'm going to take your bargain, I need a bigger fee. The sap and…" And what? What did I want from the druids? "And a boon, one that I can transfer to another if I choose."

"Your sight doesn't seem that valuable to you, wizard. Have you become so used to relying on apprentices? You are certainly gathering more of them."

I'd pissed him off. Good. "I value my sight, but what you are asking is unprecedented. Has anyone in the past been able to stop a prophecy coming true when it was time?"

"No, but the prophecy of the six has come close many times and stopped. We believe it was because someone took action. If we are right, it can be stopped again."

I didn't know if it was logic, or wishful thinking. The conditions for a prophecy this obscure would be complex, and a small thing could change the environment at the last minute. It was unlikely to be caused by someone on purpose. "Myrddin, I think you are right. I don't value my sight over a prophecy. I will not accept your bargain."

"You are making a mistake, wizard. Your refusal does not mean we will cease our efforts. You are not the only option we have."

"No, but I was the best. Lionel, show Myrddin out, and revoke his privileges." I tried to sound stern, but I was really just relieved. I could live a long time by not getting involved with the druids again.

. . .

LIONEL AND I HAD STAYED UP LATE INTO THE NIGHT ARGUING about my decision. He worried that I would lose the opportunity to regain my sight and that the druids would find someone else. Leaving Dionne in unknown danger.

I agreed. I just didn't want to let them control our actions. We could protect Dionne; someone had been doing that for her whole life. And we would find the sap another way.

Eventually, he accepted that I wouldn't change my mind, and we got some rest. At least I did. It was good to know I had a way forward. Whatever price I had to pay Moss for the sap, it would be less than what the druids wanted.

The next morning, we were waiting for Bud to arrive and the doorbell rang.

"I'll get it," Lionel said. "Maybe it's someone who can give us some sap."

I laughed, thinking it was more likely someone bringing another impossible quest.

"It's Ms. Metcalfe," Lionel called as he clomped in. "I've asked her into the kitchen for tea."

"I won't stay for tea. I don't have long, Mr. Larson." Her voice was stern. "I need to arrange a meeting and a full home inspection."

"I thought you just needed to check on the business," Lionel said. "Would you like a cookie with your tea?"

"No, as I said, I don't have time today."

Princess had a point about the oath. I realized that Lionel was pretty much able to say, or do, what he pleased. I'll have to give some more thought to that. I signaled him to let me handle the situation. "Is there a reason you need to do a full inspection?"

"Is there a reason I should be worried?"

"I was just wondering if anything has changed." My mind raced through the spells we'd need to make this whole place look... human.

"Dionne's foster parents were concerned about the late nights. There have not been that many, but it is a worrying trend, and I am responsible for her wellbeing."

"It's good to know someone is looking out for her. I'll make sure she's not staying late any more. We're pretty well set up now anyway."

"That's all well and good. I still need to inspect the whole environment. And I'll be interviewing your neighbors."

That wasn't such an easy thing to deal with. Lionel coughed, and I jumped in before he could say anything more. "When do you want to do this?"

She hesitated, or rather, she didn't answer right away, which wasn't the same thing. "I have an opening Monday at two?"

I nodded. "We'll be available."

"Ms. Metcalfe?" Lionel said. "What exactly does this inspection entail? I mean, with Quinn's handicap, we may need to do some preparation."

"It's nothing to prepare for. I'll need to see the areas of the house I haven't been in; the basement, your bedrooms. No need to worry unless you have bodies buried down there." She gave little laugh.

"No bodies." *Just a lot of power sunk into the ground from years of spell crafting.*

"I'll need to go through your garden as well. I noticed you have a lot of herbs out there."

"I think it's nice to have fresh herbs," I said. "Will you need me to get the neighbors to call?" *Please say yes.* I needed to control this.

"No. My office will contact them and set up some time. Now I must go. No need to show me out."

I held my hand up to keep Lionel from talking until I heard the front door open and close.

As soon as we were alone, he started, "Quinn, what are we going to do? The workroom has too much power in it to hold a glamour for any length of time."

"I know. We'll have to use some up by powering other things. If we go talk to Moss, maybe we can give him some of the excess in payment for sap."

"And we'll have to wait for the inspection to be done before we try to get your sight back."

Well, we needed the sap first, but he was right, my vision couldn't be miraculously restored overnight. And I had no confidence in my ability to pretend to be blind. "I guess we should be grateful that it wasn't a surprise visit. We might have been in the middle of casting a spell when she knocked. At least we have some time to prepare."

"What are we going to do about the neighbors?"

"I don't think we can do anything about it." I had a feeling we'd only make it worse. "What are they going to say? That we keep to ourselves?"

When Bud arrived, we decided to start draining the workroom. I sat on the side of the workbench while they discussed the best way to get the power level down enough so Ms. Metcalfe wouldn't get jumpy. This much energy could affect even the most insensitive of humans.

"I think we can push some of the energy into the garden," Bud said.

"Not too much. She'll go out there and inspect too," Lionel said.

It was nice to have them working together instead of bickering. I relaxed a bit. We had time to get this done as long as no other problems came along. The office was going to be tricky. A glamour with enough power to be touched would take too much

2

power to be ignored. Maybe Dionne would have an idea how to deal with that. She was our resident human expert after all.

"I could have some of the rose fairies come and take a little power away with them." Bud was doing a great job of sounding innocent, but I wasn't prepared to hand over free power to the fairies.

"Maybe another approach would be better. I don't think having fairies traipse through the house will be easily hidden from the neighbors."

"Could we push the power down?" Lionel asked. "I mean, just push it far enough away that she won't feel it, and then pull it back when she's gone?"

"How would you do that, Lionel?" Bud sounded impressed. "I do not think I have heard of this kind of spell. What is deep below this house?"

I used my foot to feel for the edge of the earth where we conducted our magic. My basement was built up around a central circle of bare soil. A few inches of sub floor wasn't much to fall over, but if I stepped wrong, I'd easily break an ankle. "I'm not sure what's down there. We'd need some bedrock to hold the power, and it would only hold it for a few days before it started to seep out."

"I can't sense much below here," Lionel said. "How can we find out?"

It felt good that I still had some lessons to give him. "I can do that. I just need quiet and time. Leave me here and go test the garden for any problems we might need to deal with before Monday."

"Are you sure?" Lionel asked.

"I'm going to send my senses down as far as I can go. Put a ward on the door when you leave. I'll be about half an hour."

"Quinn Larson, I do not like to leave you for this. What if something comes and takes your magic?"

I smiled. She was learning caution. "I'll be fine, Bud."

"Quinn Larson, why does this human need to inspect your house? Does she think you would not protect one of the six?"

"The humans don't know about the prophecy, Bud. And they can't know about it. You need to stay away on Monday."

"All day?"

"Yes. We can't risk her seeing anything she shouldn't." I realized keeping Bud away wouldn't be enough. "Lionel will set a ward around the house when Ms. Metcalfe is inside. We have to keep all Real Folk away."

"I can do that. Bud, come on. We'll check the garden. Be careful, Quinn."

"I will, don't worry. I'll show you how to do this when I can watch you." With luck that would be soon.

They left, and I felt the hush when Lionel set the ward. I sought out any other entities, remembering the last time Lionel had encountered a rogue spirit. There was nothing, and no one, in attendance.

I closed my eyes to let my mind know I was going to do focused magic.

I sat cross-legged on the earth and placed my palms flat. The earth was packed tight. It felt damp and ancient. I took in a deep breath, and as I exhaled, I let my power slide into the ground. Keeping a tendril of it attached to my mind, I let it sink deeper.

It took ten minutes for me to find rock, but when I did, I could tell it was deep and would be able to hold all the power I needed to send. It would start to leak back up as soon as we finished but doing it late Sunday night would be safe enough.

I was shaking with the need for food by the time I felt my way up the stairs and made it back to the kitchen. Letting power out for that long was a good way for a wizard to get sick.

"Lionel, do we have any oatmeal left over?"

"Quinn Larson, you look very pale. Have some of the honey you keep in that jar. I can get it for you."

"Thank you, Bud. I need something more substantial." I told them what I'd found underground. "So, we'll do it on Sunday. The power will rise back by Wednesday." I took the bowl that Lionel placed in my hand. The heat from the contents was good on my fingers.

"Let's hope we don't need it before then," Lionel said. "I've been thinking about our problem, and maybe I have a solution."

I nodded for him to continue and kept eating. The oatmeal was studded with nuts and fruit that would help speed up the recharging time.

"If we ask Moss, he might ask for a favor in return. In fact, I'm sure he will. It might be something you don't want to pay."

"Moss will not ask Quinn Larson to do anything bad." Bud sounded insulted.

"I didn't say it would be bad. I said Quinn might not want to do the favor." Lionel sounded like he was repeating an old argument. "I just mean it might be better to get someone who owes you a favor already."

"I seem to owe more people than owe me." I pushed the bowl away, full and feeling almost back to normal. "And it has to be someone who is able to get the sap."

"Yes. But that could be anyone who can get into the park. I mean a fairy could get it."

Bud squeaked in annoyance. "Lionel, I told you we cannot do this for Quinn Larson. If I could get it, I would have done that already."

I guessed they'd been arguing about this in the garden. "We know, Bud. I think Lionel is just leading up to something. Go on."

"We did a favor for the synymphs. Maybe they can bring the sap up for you."

The synymphs had come into the park a few months ago. At first, it looked like they might be responsible for the missing fairy treasure. But we'd cleared their name and I'd received a boon. "That's a great idea, Lionel. It might work. They are nymphs of a sort, so they should be able to find the oldest tree and call up some sap."

"Should I go ask?" Lionel sounded eager.

"No, Quinn Larson. What if Moss sees him and says that he cannot ask? If Moss says no, then the synymphs cannot help you. Let me go. I can sneak past Moss. He won't suspect I'm there."

Bud had a point. "Be careful," I told her. "Do you know where they are?"

"Yes, I think I can find them," she said. "Shall I go now?"

There didn't seem to be any reason to wait. If they couldn't get the sap, I would have to find another route, or settle for permanent blindness. "Don't get into any trouble while you are there, Bud."

Bud was still away by the time Dionne breezed in an hour later, chatting all the way into the kitchen. "I can't stay long. I have to go to the movies. The foster parents are making me spend time with the family tonight. They are making a big deal about me not getting enough social time."

"We know," Lionel said. "We had a visit from the social worker. You should take more care that we don't have to deal with her."

"Lionel, it's not Dionne's fault. It is what happens when you get tangled up with humans." I hoped it was just an overly conscientious social worker. "Dionne, Ms. Metcalfe is going to do a full inspection of the house."

"Oh, that's not great. How long do we have to prepare? I can ditch the movie if you need me to help. I can do whatever it takes to help you pass. Is there something that needs hiding? Or maybe I can help keep people away."

I shook my head. "No. I get the feeling that it would just make matters worse if you stayed. Apparently, you've been staying here late too often. I thought it was only the one time, but your foster parents are being protective of you, I guess."

"Oh, well," Dionne cleared her throat before continuing. "It might be my fault."

"What did you do?" Lionel asked. This time I didn't try to stop him. She deserved to answer his questions no matter what the tone.

"I had to spend some time hanging with my friends. I went to meet them a few times. I guess I stayed too late. I'm really sorry, Quinn."

"You should be," Lionel said. "We didn't need all this right now. We have to find that last ingredient for Quinn's spells, not drain the workroom or find a way to make the upstairs look like an office."

"I said I'm sorry. And anyway, didn't the druids give you that sap?" That was a nice try at diverting attention.

I held up my hand, but it seemed Lionel wasn't paying attention.

"No. They wanted Quinn to stop the prophecy, and he said no. He put you first, ahead of his sight, ahead of his safety."

"I didn't mean to —"

"Both of you stop talking." I hated to raise my voice, but Dionne had to leave soon, and this was not going to get us anywhere. "Dionne, we need your help getting the work room ready for inspection. We will deal with your behavior after this is done."

"But..."

"No buts. How can we get desks and whatever else we need for Monday?"

She sighed, and I waited for the argument, but it seemed she was willing to let things go, at least for now. "I can order a couple of cheap desks from Staples, and chairs. Where's that computer?"

Lionel brought the machine to her, and I heard them discussing the best options.

"Do you have that credit card, Quinn?"

"In my sock drawer."

A few minutes and clicks later, she said, "They will deliver Sunday. I've made a payment to the card to cover the cost. I'll be able to get everything set up, so it looks like we are in business."

"Thanks, now you should go and enjoy your movie." I was getting worried about Bud. She should have been back by now. When Dionne was gone, Lionel and I could go to the park and find her.

"I can be here by nine," she said. "But, Quinn, you should have taken the bargain. It's not that important for me to be one of the six."

I was touched. "I won't ask you to give up who you are for me. I can manage without my sight if I have to."

"But you shouldn't have to."

"The druids aren't the only source of the sap."

"I know, but, Quinn, I don't want you to suffer for me. You should get your sight back and then we can figure it out from there. I feel like I'm being a problem."

"Dionne, I don't think you are a problem. I don't know what you think I can do with my sight that I can't do without it. I won't put you at risk."

"But..."

"I couldn't take the bargain, Dionne. The prophecy needs to happen when it's ready."

"But you'll still be blind. You should be able to get your sight back. It's not fair."

It would be nice to live in a world where fair existed. "I'll find another way. Bud is trying to get what we need from another source. Right now, we have to get through this inspection on Monday and figure out the prophecy."

"But that would be easier if you could see, right?"

It would be stupid to deny it. Everything would be easier if I could see. "Go enjoy your movie. We'll get this figured out."

She kissed my cheek and then ran out.

I started to get my coat when the front door opened on a rush.

"I am back, Quinn Larson," Bud called, running into the room. "And I have wonderful news."

I smiled. Fairies would never be the subtle politicians that the sidhe were, but the joy she felt over completing a straightforward task was worth more than any beauty that Maeve could portray. "You have the sap?"

"Not yet, but soon. I had to search for them – they are very odd – and then it was hard to make them understand."

"But you were able to do it?" Lionel opened a cupboard as he spoke.

"Yes. The synymph man said that he was able to call the sap but would have to be gentle. The sap will be ready in two days." She climbed onto my lap with the last words. "Isn't that good, Quinn Larson? In two days, you will be able to see all the wonderful things in the world."

"It is good news, thank you." It was hard to get the words out through my throat, which was tight with tears. I'd tried not to believe it was so close, too much could go wrong, but knowing I would be able to see again suddenly overcame me. I rubbed at my eyes and swallowed.

"Here, Bud," Lionel said. "You must be hungry."

I smelled rich buckwheat honey. He'd opened the good stuff. She deserved it.

"I am!" She started slurping. "Thank you, Lionel."

"How will we get the sap?" The synymphs could range farther than their local cousins. We had suspected them of stealing the fairy treasure because they were seen so far from their trees. But they couldn't get as far as my house. No one had seen them venture onto paved streets, yet.

"Beacon said he would bring it. Oh, I forgot to say he was there, and he said that he would come by at night, so the humans don't see him. Is that okay? I can go find him again, if it isn't okay. You see how good I am at doing jobs." Her voice was reaching the inaudible range again.

"It should be fine. We'll have to wait until after the inspection to do the spell, but it will be good to have everything in place. Are you finished with the honey?"

"Yes, it was delicious. Thank you." She emitted a tiny burp. "I will go home now, and come back tomorrow, and help you to disguise your house. When will Dionne come by? I have missed her."

"In the morning. Tell your mother I am proud of you for finding the synymphs."

"You are? Oh, it was not that hard."

"Goodnight, Bud," Lionel said before I could speak. "We should get our rest for the next few days."

"Yes. Goodnight, Quinn Larson. Thank you for the honey, Lionel. Sleep well."

LIONEL MIGHT BE RIGHT ABOUT NEEDING OUR REST, BUT I WAS too wound up to sleep. In two days, not only would I have what I needed to restore my sight, I would have to face a human inspection of the house. I knew I was going to forget something important, and if we failed the inspection, I would have to find another way to train Dionne.

My thoughts kept spiraling around all the things that could go wrong. I took a mug of tea out to garden. There was peace to be found in the coolness of growing things, and for the first time in a long time it wasn't tinged by sadness from the grave under the tree. And it was refreshing not to have my mind assaulted by arguing apprentices for a while.

If I couldn't get sleep, I could at least try to get more information out of The Morrigan. She was the only being who seemed to have news about the prophecy. Maybe if she knew the druids were trying to stop it, she'd think it was important enough to give me something useful.

"Morrigan, are you near?" I knew the answer was no, otherwise I would either be sweating from passion or bone chilled from fear. The words were simply a way to throw her name out to the winds.

I sipped tea and enjoyed the quiet of the night. Even in the city, there were times in the deep of night when the sounds were muffled. As I got to the bitter lees in the mug, the temperature dropped, and a siren wailed its way to the hospital, echoed by a thousand past sirens, and cries of pain and loss.

"You called me, wizard?"

A brush of wings came close enough to my skin to stop my heart. A touch of The Morrigan's feathers could kill you or, as it had with Olan, transform you. When I gathered my wits again, I wet my lips and started the conversation. "I was wondering if you were aware that the druids asked me to stop the prophecy."

"I was not aware. It is worrying any time the druids become involved in affairs outside the museum. Did they say why?" Her voice shifted from a dry creak to a warm caress.

I tried to ignore the passion that rose with the change in her voice, and told her about the souls still being restless, and the sap we needed – I needed. "I anticipate the problems in front of me will be gone by Tuesday. I can concentrate on Dionne's training. I hoped you could shed some light on the prophecy beyond what I already know?"

"I am not your servant to gather information for you, wizard."

I felt my breath ice as it left my body. There was no threat in her tone, but I didn't want to take a chance of stirring her anger. Not being able to see her was a benefit because it minimized the impact of her... well her being her. "I know. I just thought that you had some special knowledge. Perhaps I was wrong, and you don't, but I am desperate. I may have to take my chances with the druids."

"Nice flattery, Quinn. I do not have any more information for you, but I may be able to provide you with a way to contact someone who does. That is if I think you deserve my help. I fear you will be faced with this prophecy soon, and regardless of what I wish, it seems that you are in the center of everything."

I wanted to ask her what she meant, but the longer I was in her presence the more she scared me.

"Wait for me to return, wizard. Do not call me again, or I might decide to take you with me, and let the world find its own way forward. After all, I thrive on death and birth. Peace is of no use to me."

The air became cooler, and the silence was replaced by another siren and a few shouts from the street. A neighbor's dog barked, and I started to drowse. She must have drained a little of my life force to show that she had power over me. I was too cold to stay outside long, and I didn't know if she meant she was coming back this evening, or this year, or even this century. I was just considering a dash inside for a coat when the temperature rose again.

"Hold out your hand, wizard." I obeyed without speaking. Paper landed in my palm; I closed my fingers around it gently. "Now you have all I know. Use the information wisely, Quinn. You make my existence interesting. I think we have more to do together."

The heat was sucked out of the air as she left. I didn't feel much like staying out now that she was gone. I locked the back door and placed my mug in the sink. The paper was still between my fingers.

I walked to Lionel's door and raised my hand to knock. The message might be urgent, or it might be something completely useless. I hoped she wasn't playing games.

I decided it could wait until I was able to read it because Lionel needed his sleep. If The Morrigan wanted me to know the information now, she wouldn't have given a blind wizard a written note.

I turned away and stumbled into my own bedroom. I put the paper on my night table and flopped into bed. I couldn't take any more disappointment. If the note said anything other than *the information is here*, I'm not sure I could take it. I closed my eyes, and let the night take me.

❦ 19 ❦

Sunday, Dionne and Bud chattered their way into the kitchen just as we were finishing breakfast.

"The truck should be here by ten," Dionne said. "It won't take us more than an hour to set things up. I made a website for you last night. Don't worry, I did my homework first. No one will suspect anything. I made a twitter account, and a Facebook page, too."

"What are those?" Lionel beat me to the question. I had given up trying to follow the human trends years ago.

"It's how business gets done these days. I'll keep everything running enough to look like you are legit without attracting too many followers."

I trusted her, or rather, I didn't know what to do about it, so I let the subject be. "When we've set up the office, we can try the new spells you got from Fionuir's book."

"I was thinking about that," Dionne said. "Shouldn't we just try to copy all the spells? It's not like she's asking for it back. I mean does anyone know we have it?"

"Yes, Quinn Larson. You should make the most of the time

you have with the book. I can get more webs. If my clan collects them, we could go through the entire book in one day."

I was tempted. Fionuir might not agree, but she owed me. No matter how much I might justify it, in my gut, it didn't feel right stealing her spells. "I think we should give it to Maeve. It's sidhe business. We don't need the grief of getting caught doing something they might not like just to satisfy our curiosity."

"There can't be any harm in keeping it until you have your sight back," Lionel said. "I could take it back to Maeve after we do that. I mean, what if the spell doesn't work. We might have to find a new one."

His argument was persuasive. I couldn't deny it was tempting me. I had to be the adult, though. If I wanted Dionne to learn where the lines between right and wrong were in our world, I needed to stay on the right side. "I'll think about it." Then the doorbell rang, and I didn't have to start a lecture on the ethics of spell gathering.

"I'll get it," Dionne said. "Bud, go hide for a bit."

I heard her chatting to someone at the door and then boots clomping down the hall.

"That's right, just go up the stairs, and drop everything off in the room."

I froze. Dionne had given the deliverymen access to the house. Had Bud managed to hide?

Lionel touched my hand. "It's fine. Everything looks normal, at least normal to humans. Bud's in the cupboard under the sink."

I relaxed marginally. "Make sure Dionne takes any permissions back when they leave."

Three trips up the stairs and everything was delivered. Dionne asked me for some money to tip the delivery guys. I had Lionel find my wallet and give it to her.

The door banged shut after them and Lionel's voice came down the hallway. "You never give anyone permission to enter the house without checking. They could have left the boxes in the hall."

"Yes. And then we'd waste time carting everything up ourselves. You live here. You get to do magic all the time. I don't."

"Princess, you can come out now." I waved Lionel and Dionne to the stools at the counter. "We need to talk about this."

"But, Quinn, I didn't let them into anything they shouldn't. I—"

I held up my hand and she stopped speaking. "You were careful, that's not the problem. I needed to know what was happening. You almost gave me a heart attack when I realized they were going upstairs."

"I didn't think of that. Sorry."

"Don't be angry with her, Quinn Larson. She didn't think. I know that is a bad thing." Her voice cracked, and I knew she was thinking of her friends. "But nothing happened."

"We were lucky," I said. "Next time, you need to tell us what you plan, Dionne. If they had seen anything... No, I'm not going to worry about the might haves. Let's get the office set up." I stood and headed for the stairs. "I might not be able to build furniture, but I can move things around and, at least, make tea."

IT TOOK A COUPLE OF HOURS TO GET THREE DESKS AND CHAIRS put together. Dionne turned on the laptops and after a few clicks declared them ready for inspection.

"Lunch, then spells," I said. "Good work. Maybe we can find a real use for this furniture when Ms. Metcalfe is finished with us."

Lionel clomped down the stairs after us. "I'll heat the soup, and then we can start practice. In the workroom? Will it be okay? It won't affect your ability to push the power down tonight?"

I shook my head to dismiss his concern. "We'll be fine as long as we only cast a few times."

The food was welcome. I was starving from pushing furniture

around. The others must have been even more ready for sustenance. "Dionne, starting Tuesday, I need you to learn the history of the Real Folk."

"Aw, I was hoping you had forgotten that. Spells are way more fun."

I agreed, but she showed a lack of caution that needed to be dealt with. "We'll keep it light. You'll do spells as well, but you seem to catch on pretty fast with that. The history is important."

"Yes, Dionne, it is important. I learned about being a leader, and I think you will need to do that too. The six are powerful, and if you just make magic all the time, things will get bad," Bud said. "I can tell you stories to make the fairy history interesting."

"I gather the fairy stories we get from movies aren't real history," Dionne said over the sound of her spoon scraping the bowl.

I didn't know what the modern stories were like, but I liked Bud's idea. Maybe we could enlist Real Folk to tell their history. I just didn't know how to explain why she needed it. "Some of the old stories you might know are based on real events. We haven't always been so separate from the humans. There have been times when, in small areas, the lines have blurred."

"If everyone is finished eating," Lionel said. "Maybe we can go down and start practice?"

"I'll clean up later before I leave," Dionne offered. "It's the least I can do. Lionel, maybe you can tell me stories about wizard history."

I let them go ahead of me. I still made my way around slowly, and they were eager to get started. At the bottom of the stairs, I bumped into Lionel's back. "What's going on?"

"Quinn, the workroom is not going to pass inspection," Dionne said.

My heart stopped. We only had today to make this work. "What happened? It was cleared of magic things, has someone disturbed it?"

She sighed. "No, it's fine, for a wizard's workshop. There are jars of things everywhere. Things that can't easily be explained, like this jar of pickled ears."

Lionel stepped aside and let me into the room. He guided me to the sofa before speaking. "What does it need to look like?"

"Hmm, well. The easiest thing to deal with is probably the pit in the floor. We can fill it with the cardboard boxes from upstairs. It will save us figuring out how to get rid of them. Is there a way to make them look like they are sitting on the floor? Like there's no pit?"

I nodded, but let Lionel work it out with her.

"Yes, a glamour, and a levitation spell. If we make sure the boxes fill the space, she won't need to walk in there."

"Okay, that's good," she continued. "If we put all the jars in the pit, the same spell will cover them. The books are probably okay, as long as she doesn't want to read them. But that would be weird, no one starts reading a stranger's books."

"Can you show us what it should look like?" Bud asked.

"I guess I could draw it?" Dionne sounded doubtful.

"No. If you can make an image in your mind, I can use a fairy spell to make it show in the air." Bud snapped her fingers. "But first, I need you to promise you will not use the spell. It is a secret, and I would get into trouble if you used it."

We all promised. I made a mental note to suggest Lionel find a similar spell in our records. It would come in very handy for training Dionne.

Dionne sat on the sofa next to me. Bud hummed a quiet song, much more pleasant than her singing. "Dionne, you must think of the room as if you were coming down the stairs." She returned to humming.

A gasp broke my concentration on the tune.

"That's exactly what it should look like," Dionne said, wonder in her voice. "That is so perfect, Bud."

"It is easy when you know the spell," Bud couldn't hide the joy in her voice. "Now, Lionel, can you make this happen?"

"I'll get the boxes. We'll need to create a glamour to make it look like there are about three times as many. We can put the real boxes in front so if she wants to touch them, it will feel right."

I waved for their attention. "We'll do it before you leave, Dionne. Now let's get to spell practice. Perhaps we can do a few summoning spells. That way not all the boxes need to be carried by hand."

20

We spent the rest of the day acting as normal as possible. Lionel and Dionne practiced the new spells until they were letter perfect. And a few of the local mice experienced a lost hour or two as a result of the experiments.

Bud had shared some of her tribe's history. I think Dionne walked away from that with a very different view of fairies. Beacon dropped off the sap and promised to find time to tell Dionne about sprites.

When Bud left, I reminded her to stay away until tomorrow night. "I will, Quinn Larson. Besides, the council is deciding tomorrow on whether I will be my mother's heir. I will be too busy to come."

Before I could say anything, she patted my cheek, and ran out. I wished her luck.

I'd waited until late at night to push the power into the bedrock. The little power that the glamours needed wouldn't be noticed under casual inspection.

Now, Lionel and I were waiting for Ms. Metcalfe to arrive.

Me, with my stomach twisting in knots, and Lionel, silent but fidgety. "It's going to be okay, Lionel." I tried to believe the words myself, but my nerves wouldn't settle. Too many things could go wrong.

"I know, Quinn," he said. The doorbell chimed. "Oh, that must be her."

When he greeted her at the door, Lionel spoke loud enough for me to hear. "Quinn is in the kitchen, Ms. Metcalfe. I'm sure he's ready to show you the whole house."

Good that worked as we planned. I felt the slight pressure that tied me to her. She wouldn't be able to wander around alone. Now he would set the ward that would keep anyone from dropping by until she left.

"Good afternoon, Mr. Larson."

"Welcome, Ms. Metcalfe. Can we offer you some refreshment?"

"No, thank you all the same. I have another appointment to go to after this. I always have another appointment, it seems. Let's get started, shall we? I'm sure this won't take long."

I led her to the office. "As you can see, we've finally received our furniture and equipment."

"Yes, it looks good. Mr. Larson. Which desk is Dionne's?"

I had no idea if there was a right answer. Lionel saved me by saying, "The one with the pictures of her family. We like her to feel at home."

"Very well. Let's me check the facilities."

I heard a door open and then close. We'd stocked a bathroom with items Dionne had brought. Beside it, there was a small kitchen counter. If I remembered correctly, there was a kettle and a small fridge.

"You'll need to provide a fire extinguisher, but other than that, this space looks acceptable. Shall we go to the basement?"

Lionel led the way downstairs. I felt a little of the tension leave me. If the office was acceptable, we were halfway there. I figured the main floor was normal enough since she hadn't commented before. And my neighbors would probably have mentioned something if the garden was weird.

"That's a lot of boxes, Mr. Larson. Are they all full?"

I heard her knock on a box. "The ones in the front are empty. We'll be disposing of them soon. The ones in the back are full of old books, and such."

There was no answer for a second and I tensed, if she moved any of the front boxes, the illusion was all that stopped her falling into the pit. Was it normal that someone would move boxes? I had no way to understand the rules.

"Ms. Metcalfe," Lionel said. "Is there anything to be concerned about? We can clear out most of this if you prefer." I wondered where Lionel had learned to bluff so well.

"No, it's fine," Ms. Metcalfe finally said. "Although storing books in the basement is not good for the paper."

"Of course," Lionel said. "It's quite humid, but we've had no time to sort them out. I'm sure we'll get to it before it's too late."

I was starting to worry that I was standing there looking like the village idiot. I couldn't think of anything to say, and she wasn't speaking to give me something to build on.

"That's quite a long checklist. Is there anything on there we need to show you particularly?" Lionel asked.

"Oh, this is a generic list. I'm just making sure that I'm not missing something. I'm sure you don't want me coming back for a missed tick box." She gave a little laugh that was probably meant to reassure us. All it did was make me worry there would be so many boxes to tick we'd never get through this.

"Now, just the garden, and then we are done. Your neighbors were happy to provide references, although they all said you've kept more to yourself lately. Is there something I need to know?"

"Losing my sight has been a difficult adjustment. Lionel tries, but there is so much to do."

She shuffled some papers. I think I made her uncomfortable when I mentioned the blindness. "Yes, I can imagine. Well, let's get to the garden."

When we stepped out the back door, I was surprised it was raining. Surprised, but relieved. The rain would cut short the inspection.

"Oh, it's a good thing I came prepared." I heard the pop of an umbrella opening. "I can manage by myself if you don't want to get wet, Mr. Larson."

"Lionel will come with you. He knows the garden better than I do. I don't want to trip on anything in this rain." I went back to the kitchen.

A few minutes later, they both joined me. "Well that's all of it, I think. Let me just update the checklist." She made a few mmhmm noises as her pen scratched at the paper. "Yes. Everything has passed."

"Does that mean Dionne can come back to work?" I hadn't thought about the fact that she'd have to stay away. I mean I knew it, but it sank in just as Ms. Metcalfe announced us clear.

"Oh yes, just make sure she is home by nine o'clock, and doesn't let her homework fall behind. I think it's good that she has some responsibility. I usually have to work hard in the last few months of my role with my kids. Dionne has taken on the responsibility of getting herself ready to leave our care. I have a lot of confidence that she'll make something important of herself. There's something about her."

What did she mean by leave her care? "I thought she has a couple of years before she comes out of foster care."

"Oh, she had a birthday a few months ago. Well, I say birthday, but she was a few weeks old when she came into care. We picked a day and that's what's in the record as her birthday. I know most of my charges are so anxious to get into the adult world that they feel the last few months are like a lifetime. I do worry that they will just fall into the wrong path. I try to keep in touch, but it never works." She sounded truly concerned.

"From what I've seen, you care a lot. Are you sure you don't want some tea?"

"Goodness no. I'll have to rush to get to my next meeting. Good luck in your new business, Mr. Larson."

"Quinn Larson, Quinn Larson. They said yes. They said I could be the queen when my mother is dead."

Bud wrapped her arms around my leg and squeezed. "I am glad of that, Bud. Let us hope your mother lives a long life."

"Oh yes. She says she is feeling very strong today. Why is Lionel carrying the boxes to the backyard?"

"We passed the inspection, and now we don't need the boxes. He'll send them away tonight."

"So, we all had good luck today. That is a good sign for tonight, yes? Three lucks in a row." She pulled on my pant leg. "I have brought tears. They are tears of happiness, which may be better than just ordinary tears."

"I hope so." I wouldn't let myself feel hope, or fear, about the spell.

"Hey, Quinn," Dionne said. "I heard that you made it through Ms. Metcalfe's inquisition. So, let's get to the workshop and bring back your sight."

"Not so fast, Dionne. You had a birthday?"

"Oh, yeah. A while back. I didn't know you then. Why? I mean, it's no big deal."

Her shell always surprised me. At that age, it was part of the veneer, but with Dionne, it felt defensive, almost as if it was part of her protection. It must have served her well as she grew up, but a good witch needed to be closer to her feelings. "You'll be out of government care in a few months. It would have been good to know."

"Why? Would it have changed anything? I didn't realize that we could put stuff off."

I let it go. There was no need to get into a fight with her about a missed birthday. "When I have my sight back, we can have a little celebration. We'll call it your first witch birthday." And by then, she would have realized that she would be free of the system soon. We'd be having arguments about her moving in.

She slid her arm around mine and tugged me toward the stairs. "Sure, now let's do this. You need to be able to see."

A minute later, I sat in the center of the dirt floor. Bud held my left hand, patting it from time to time. The earth was damp from the rain and would stay that way until the power finished rising from the stone to warm it dry.

"Okay, Quinn," Lionel said. "We'll prepare the first spell and then put it on your face. Are you ready?"

I nodded.

Bud squeezed my hand. "It will work, Quinn Larson."

I took a deep breath and let it out. "It will be fine, Bud. Whether it works or not, it will be fine."

I smelled sage and heard a mortar and pestle. "I'm going to put this on your eyes now, Quinn," Dionne said. "Just close your eyes and hold still."

The mixture was cold against my eyelids and I could sense light filtering through. I had to force myself not to blink open my eyes and spoil the spell.

An age later, Lionel said, "Just a few more minutes, Quinn."

The sound of fabric tearing was the next indication of progress. Then some quiet words.

"Okay," Dionne said. "This will be cold, but when I've wiped it away, you should be able to see."

She was gentle, but the liquid burned. All I could do was concentrate on not reacting. I worried about crushing Bud's hand, but I wanted the contact. In my heart, I wanted to believe this would work. In my head, I couldn't stop the worst-case scenarios running; it wouldn't work, it would make things worse, it would take something else in payment.

"Okay, it's clear. You can open your eyes," Dionne's voice cut through my panic.

"Quinn, you can open your eyes," Lionel repeated.

I felt Bud's hand slip from mine. Then she stepped on my knee. Suddenly tiny fingers were prizing open my eyelids. "See, Quinn Larson, it is easy."

I looked into her eyes. A grin crossed her face, showing pointed teeth from cheek to cheek.

22

"You see me!" She kissed my cheek and started dancing around the room. "We did it. We cured Quinn Larson!" Then she started singing, and I had to cover my ears.

"Wow, that's harsh, Bud," Dionne said.

I looked at her for the first time since we took her in. The only previous sight I'd had of her was with the aid of a temporary spell. She was beautiful, long blond hair, and fair skin. There was a touch of the sidhe about her, but I thought it must be part of the glamour. No other feeling of sidhe came to me. My memory of the glance I'd had in the bar must have changed because she looked more complete, more real. "There's something different about you."

She frowned. "What do you mean?"

"Yes. I was going to mention that," Lionel said. "I noticed the protective glamour has been draining the last week, or so. It didn't change her looks, so I think it was a memory spell. I think it stopped people remembering details. Like they'd remember her but couldn't really describe her."

"That would make sense. Much easier to maintain in secret," I said. "That kind of glamour can be set with some parameters so that trusted people will remember her features. I guess we can be trusted."

Lionel just nodded and started to clear the circle. I noticed a touch of age on his face, a few lines around his eyes, and a tightening of his mouth. Taking care of me must have been wearing on him. At least we could change our relationship to apprentice and teacher. "Leave the circle intact for now. I have something else for us to try."

I pulled the paper that The Morrigan had given me from my pocket. The words were scratched in brown ink on faded paper. "This should give us some information on the prophecy. That's our only priority right now."

Bud stopped singing and came to rest in front of me. "Let me see that, Quinn Larson."

I held it out to her, but kept it in my hands. She turned her head sideways then back the other way. "I do not know how to read it."

She was so anxious to help I had to smile. "Then it's a good thing I do. It will summon a particular spirit. I think we'll be able to ask questions, but mostly it will tell us what it knows."

Lionel came to look over my shoulder. "Are you going to do it now?"

I wanted to say yes, to use my sight now that I had it back, but I had a responsibly to teach Lionel and Dionne. I forced myself to say, "You are going to do it, you and Dionne. I think you can lead her through it. Bud and I will watch."

They both lit up at the thought of doing such grand magic. Summoning an unknown entity was more than routine summoning. Lionel taking the lead with another student, when I could easily have taught her, was the first step in his graduation to wizard. He didn't seem to realize I was starting to let him go.

He would make a good teacher because his thoughts were all about his student. I could learn something from him.

I looked at the instructions on the page again. "You'll need to go get honey from the kitchen and warm it. Grass from the back-yard, cut it from the side of the lavender patch. And a jewel, I'm not sure we have any." My stock was paste and other fake jewelry.

"I can give you this one," Dionne said, pulling off her ring. "It's tiny, but it's a real diamond. I got it from a craft place."

The ring was a plain silver band with a sliver of diamond in the center. "You don't have to give us something like that."

She dropped the ring into the center of the circle. "I don't need it anymore. It's a Goth thing."

I nodded, even though I didn't have a clue what she meant and turned back to the page. "Bring some cinnamon bark. We'll need to burn it. That's all."

Lionel opened the circle and waved Dionne through. Bud and I waited the few minutes it took them to gather the ingredients. I put my hand on the earth and tested how much power had returned to the surface. Not that much, I would have to pour a bit of my own in for this spell. "Bud, I need you to keep an eye out for intrusions."

"I can do that, Quinn Larson. I am very excited about learning the truth about the prophecy."

"You can't tell anyone what we learn, Bud."

She winked at me. "I know. Leaders sometimes need to keep secrets."

"I think your training is complete."

The grin dropped from her face. "But I can still come here, Quinn Larson. I want to stay with my new friends."

"You are always welcome, Bud. But you will need to be more involved in your tribe."

Tears formed on her eyelashes. "I know, but I will miss Dionne and Lionel."

I put my hand on the ground before I spoke. "They will come to visit you."

She drooped a little and nodded for me to go ahead. I slipped the power from my fingertips into the ground just enough to power the protective circle. When I finished, I saw Lionel and Dionne hurrying down the stairs, hands full of ingredients.

They followed my instructions and we sat waiting for what felt like an eternity but was probably only a few minutes. Then a voice, dry and ancient, called out. "Who summons me from my rest?"

"Lionel, apprentice to Quinn."

He could have named me as the contact, but I had given them the spell to cast, so I kept my mouth shut and watched. Dionne was sitting cross-legged facing Lionel, her eyes closed, their fingers touching.

"What is it that you would know, Lionel apprentice to Quinn?"

I held my breath. We had no idea how many questions it would allow.

"The prophecy of the six, we want to know what it says."

"Ah, the time must be nearing again."

"The details?"

"Persistent. Good, you will need that. The prophecy states that when the six come together the world will change. There will be danger, opportunity, and fear. Those trapped will find freedom. Those who are afraid will find courage. Those in power may fail. The six are now born and they are starting to come together."

It was more than we knew, but I would have preferred something more along the lines of 'a treasure lost will be found at 123 Main Street at four o'clock next Friday' but that's prophecy for you.

Lionel glanced at me and then asked, "Do you know who is trapped?"

"I have told you all that I know. Now I will return to my rest." The offerings sank into the ground, and I felt the presence drift away.

Lionel released Dionne's hands and started to clear the circle. Bud left my side to talk to Dionne and I stood to shake out the stiffness of sitting on the ground. "I don't know if that was any help," I said.

"Information is good," Lionel said. Then he jerked. "There's —"

I felt the chill of the grave. Something was invading the circle. I tried to reach out to Bud and Dionne to protect them, but I was frozen.

"It is dangerous to continue," a whisper came from the center of the dirt floor. It was the same voice that warned me about trying to find Dionne's parents. I relaxed a little. This was no threat. "He is coming... I..."

The voice faded, but I still couldn't move. Then another voice filled the circle. It spoke in an ancient language, the words hard and raspy. I knew it, but no one else would understand the threat coming, it was casting a death spell.

"Get away from us," I screamed. "Lionel, protect Dionne and Bud. It is trying to kill."

I saw Dionne speaking, and she flung a hand toward Lionel. He tossed Bud an acorn that I knew held a shield. I still couldn't move, but I needed to protect Lionel. The words came to a conclusion and Lionel dropped to the ground boneless. Dionne's eyes rolled back in her head, and she collapsed alongside him. I had to save one of them. I had the spell from the druids, I shouted *Mnemonic* hoping that they hadn't lied. Mist flew from my fingers and settled on Dionne. She jerked in a breath.

The presence fled, and my body started to respond to my commands. I rushed to Dionne's side. She was alive. Bud flew to touch her. "She is far away, Quinn Larson, but she is coming back."

My heart started beating again, and then stopped when I looked at Lionel. His body was still. I sent my senses to find his spirit, but there was nothing. I could sense no warmth in his skin, no sense of his spirit in the shell that was left on the floor of my workroom.

Another life wasted because of my actions. I was dangerous to my friends.

My legs gave out, and I felt the pain as my knees slammed into the earth. Had I opened a portal when I placed my power in the circle? I knew there would be a price for my sight. I would never have paid the price of Lionel's life just to be able to see.

"Quinn Larson, do not die too." Bud's tears hit my arm. "They need you. Dionne is crying. She needs you. Quinn Larson, please come back."

I reached out to Lionel to say goodbye, but my hand could not make contact. Then I heard Dionne muttering as though she was speaking to someone. If she were possessed, I would have to work fast. I couldn't waste the spell I'd cast to save her.

I crawled across the floor to reach her. Bud tried to help me stand, but she was too small to lift me. "Don't hurt yourself. I need you to help me with Dionne."

She ran to Dionne's side. "What do I have to do?"

I reached for Dionne's hand and felt a twitch of the muscles.

"She's trying to come back. I need to you to call her, while I search for the path."

Bud started to sing again, this time I heard the music as well as the screech. My vision blurred, was I going to be blind again? Was nothing going to go right? Then I realized it was tears as they burned down my cheeks. *Crying isn't going to solve this, idiot.*

Taking a deep breath, I reached for Dionne's spirit. Bud was right. She was far away. I felt her draw closer as I tried to find a way to connect with her spirit to bring her back.

There was only darkness beyond her body; a vast darkness that sapped my own spirit as I searched for a glimpse of energy.

Then a light glinted, and I cast my spirit toward it and found a thread of Dionne's spirit. I reached for Bud. "Can you feel this?"

"Yes, I can guide her, Quinn Larson. You can let me guide her."

I was shaking with the effort of holding onto Dionne. I helped Bud reach for the link. It was already stronger than it had been at first. I disconnected as soon as Bud held it. The power that I had sunk into the earth would have helped me now, but it was spent.

"I have her, Quinn Larson," Bud whispered. "Why is she crying? Who is she talking to?"

"I don't know Bud, maybe she can tell us when she wakes."

I tested the link between fairy and witch, it was strong enough for me to leave them. Apparently, the druids had not lied about the spell. They hadn't been entirely truthful, but it didn't matter. Dionne was alive and on her way back.

"I need to check on Lionel. Dionne did something to him. I need to make sure he's at rest."

I kept pushing myself to take the next action, to not think about what happened. I needed to keep moving. This time I knew how to put my grief aside and function.

I felt again for power in the soil, but it was all gone. The old power was rising, but it would be days before it settled back. Someone, or something, was trying to make sure we couldn't recover from this attack. Had they attacked because the power was low? Was it just coincidence? Had The Morrigan known something like this was going to happen?

I crawled across to Lionel. There was still some kind of shell around him, but I could reach inside if I worked slowly. When I had enough of myself inside, I tested for life. His body wasn't dead, but there was no spirit. Whatever Dionne had done, I would have to wait until she regained consciousness to find out what we could do about it.

I would have to leave his body where it was until I knew whether to bury him, or not.

24

"She is coming back, Quinn Larson." Bud's announcement broke through my exhaustion. "She is talking."

I shook off the daze, and managed to stand, and walk to where Dionne was groaning and rolling over. Her color was returning, and as I neared, her eyes opened.

Her gaze locked on my face and she bolted upright. "Is he safe?"

"Lionel's body is there," I said pointing behind me. "I don't know if he's safe. Are you okay?"

Bud fluttered back to Dionne's side. "I was so worried about you. Who were you talking to? Where were you?"

Dionne gave a reassuring smile to Bud. "I was safe. The Morrigan was there. She told me how to get back. She helped me. She said she wasn't ready to take me, yet."

Maybe The Morrigan had taken Lionel somewhere safe too. "You need to go home soon. Can you walk? We'll get some food into you to give you some strength before you go."

She stood and walked to where Lionel's body was stretched out on the floor. "Can we move him somewhere warmer? The damp won't be good for him. It might be a while before we can figure out how to reverse this."

We lifted him and placed Lionel on the couch. I would bring a blanket down later. "You can tell us what you did over a bowl of soup."

I ushered them both upstairs. Bud held Dionne's hand as though she could keep her safe just by contact.

I heated the soup, my emotions hiding behind the mundane tasks. I let Dionne eat most of it before I started asking questions.

"I saw you cast a spell before the attack, what was it?"

She swallowed the spoonful of broth. "I knew you would save me. I saw it on your face. I used that time slowing spell, and the one to send his spirit somewhere safe."

Too fast, if she could do what she said she'd just done, then I had no hope of training her at my pace. She would devour the knowledge she wanted and ignore anything she didn't value. Too fast, and too dangerous. "Did you and Lionel practice those spells?"

"I just memorized them. I can do that. I just memorize stuff I want to remember." She swallowed more of the broth, color returning to her face. "Quinn, I knew if it came to a choice, you would sacrifice Lionel for me. I don't think you would get over that. You didn't get over Cate, and you wouldn't get over Lionel. I didn't want to be the reason Lionel died. So, I figured I would get something ready."

I didn't know what else to say, so I just nodded for her to finish the soup.

"Quinn Larson, do not be angry with Dionne. She did a good thing." Bud turned to stare wide-eyed at Dionne. "You made two spells so quickly? You are very powerful. I am glad you are my friend."

Dionne shrugged and finished her soup. "When can we start searching for Lionel's spirit? I think I can reverse the spell and put him back together, but I need to know where he is. Let's get back to him."

"You have to go home, Dionne. We can't have another visit from the social worker. Lionel will be fine until tomorrow."

"No. We have to find his spirit." She jumped up and started toward the workroom. "How do you know we will be able to put his spirit back if we wait?"

I held her arm. "I will research it tonight. Now that I can see, I can be more useful with that. I need you to go home. I need you to be normal until you get back here. Lionel needs you to do this. If people get suspicious, we'll have to waste time covering up what we're doing."

She was shaking, but I held her until she looked at me. "Okay, but this is a priority, Quinn. I don't care about the prophecy. I want Lionel back."

"We'll get him back," I said. "I'm not letting him go either. But we need to be smart. Don't do anything to bring Ms. Metcalfe back here. We need time to work this out. You did the right thing."

"Don't fight," Bud shouted. "You are wasting time fighting. Quinn Larson is right, Dionne. Go home. Don't bring the humans back. I will ask my council to find information. I will get webs for Quinn so he can read more of the book tonight. We will find answers."

I felt Dionne let go of her panic, then her muscles relaxed under my hand. She nodded, reluctantly. "I'll be back right after school." She looked closely at my face. "You look like death warmed over. I can't fix this by myself, get some rest."

The authority in her voice was new. She'd changed from a teenager to an adult over the course of those two spells she'd cast. She pulled her arm from my grasp and picked up her coat and bag.

. . .

AFTER DIONNE LEFT, BUD AND I WENT TO HARVEST WEBS. WE found ten in my garden and she promised to have her tribe bring more tomorrow. I sent her home. She should spend time with her mother before Princess faded completely away. I didn't find anything useful in Fionuir's book, so I pulled down all of my spell books, falling asleep over them just as the dark began to lift. When I woke, Bud was sitting beside me laying more webs out. I pushed myself up and stretched.

"Good morning, Quinn Larson. Were you successful?"

"No, but I think we can just call his spirit through a circle. And maybe one of the other spirits will know something if we can't get Lionel's to come."

"My mother is gone."

There was no emotion in her words. Fairies were creatures of emotion, joy, anger, fear; this was eerie and unwelcome. "I am sorry, Bud. That must be painful."

"I have already cried for her. I am sad, but sadness will not help find Lionel." She looked up from the webs she'd arranged on the counter. I saw the pain in her eyes. "Let us start using these webs. My fairies will bring more throughout the day. I think we will need a hundred."

I pulled Fionuir's book out from under a pile of others. "We can do this faster if we don't write down any of the ones that don't relate to what we need."

"It is a pity to waste the webs, but perhaps when we have Lionel back, we can do this all again." She wiped a tear from her eye.

"I think Lionel would want us to have tea first, or rather honey for you and tea for me." I piled the books to the side and put the kettle on.

Fionuir's book was full of interesting spells, most I'd never heard of before. I itched to write them down, but I couldn't tell Dionne that we'd wasted time on a spell to sweeten the air, or one to call hummingbirds.

We stopped for a quick lunch, and to check on Lionel periodically. There was no change. Throughout the day, Rose fairies dropped off webs. By early afternoon we'd been through the entire book and found nothing that allowed us to find a wandering spirit.

"I think we're left with the same options that I had before we started."

She yawned. "Yes, Quinn Larson it seems so."

I was finding it difficult to keep my eyes open too. "Dionne will be here in an hour or so, let's get some rest."

"No. We can prepare the circle. We can make the spirit gifts. We can..."

I held up my hand. "Sleep for a few minutes. Then we can prepare. I can't fall asleep during the search."

DIONNE ARRIVED AS WE WERE PLACING THE LAST OF THE SPIRIT offerings in the circle. I heard her stomping across the room upstairs, a thud of something hitting the floor preceded her run down the stairs to join us. "What do we know? Did you find a spell?"

She looked like she hadn't slept. Her hair was pulled back into a braid, wisps sticking out everywhere. Her eyes were red, her skin pale.

"We are going to have to call through the spirit world," I said, pointing for her to sit on one of the cushions we'd placed on the still damp ground. "We'll start by trying to call Lionel directly. If that doesn't work, we'll call some of the spirits I know for information."

"Okay, let's get started."

"I need to know you will do as I say. If we have to talk to other spirits, you must be silent. If they get you to talk, they'll know who you are. We can't let that happen."

"Yes, Dionne, you must be careful. A spirit could try to steal you if they know." Bud swept a few grains of chalk away from the circle. "We must find Lionel. If you are stolen, we will have to stop and find you."

"I promise to be quiet. Let's get started."

I closed the circle and placed a mug of Lionel's favorite tea in the center. "Lionel, if you can hear my voice come to the circle."

I felt Bud and Dionne add their own power to my call. We waited. After a few minutes, I put the call out again. "Lionel, if your spirit is near, provide us a sign."

I watched the mug. Liquid was an easy element for spirits to move. When nothing happened for five minutes, I turned to Dionne. "Try to call him. Maybe you'll have a tie to him because of the spell."

She looked over my shoulder at Lionel's body lying on the couch. "Lionel, I am sorry I sent you away. Please answer the call."

The water rippled. I nodded to her to try again.

"Lionel, please talk to us, we need to know where you are."

"Dionne?" he answered, his voice was weak, but he answered.

"Yes, Lionel. Where are you?"

"It's cold here."

"Help us bring you back. Where should we look?"

Dionne glanced at me. I nodded encouragement. "Keep him talking."

"Can you see anything?"

"Cold and dark."

"Can you hear anything? Or is there something that will tell us where you are?"

"There are others."

Bud glance up from where she sat, hands on the ground. "Ask him to describe the others, Dionne."

"Hooded... Angry."

"Can you come back?" she asked.

"I can't find a way out. I think these are druids." His voice became more certain. "Dionne, I think I am in the Gur amulet."

"Ask him if he is in danger," I said.

"No, I don't think they are aware I'm here. If I'm in the amulet, there isn't a way out."

"We'll find one, Lionel. I promise you we will find a way to get you out. I wish I had thought of something else to save you."

"No. Don't waste your time. I won't answer again. Leave me here and work on the prophecy. Goodbye."

"Lionel. Lionel?" Dionne screamed.

I closed down the summoning and broke the circle.

"Dionne, it's useless. If he won't answer, you can't force it."

She shuddered and tears streamed down her face. Bud wrapped her arms around the girl. "We will still try to free him, won't we, Quinn. Don't cry, Dionne."

"There will be a way, Dionne. The druids will know a way, or someone else. We'll keep trying."

I hoped I was speaking the truth.

WANT MORE?

Quinn's world is out of control. Use the QR code to grab your copy of Imbalance and watch his reality fly out of control.

Sneak peek next

If you enjoyed reading Obsession, please consider helping other readers to find the story by leaving a review.

CHAPTER 1

"Quinn, we aren't getting anywhere." Dionne's voice pulled my attention away from the sight of Lionel's body lying on the sofa. Having my sight back was a benefit, but there were some things I could live without seeing. Lionel's lifeless body was one of those things. His lanky frame looked skeletal without life giving it purpose. His red hair looked flat rather than the wild mess it normally ended up in.

"If you don't concentrate, we won't get him back." She poked me, and I came close to telling her that the apprentice doesn't hurt the master, but she was right, and I'm not that kind of wizard. Her hair was drawn back into a ponytail, and she seemed to have aged in the last week beyond her seventeen years. Her green eyes blazed out of dark rings of exhaustion.

"Okay, let me cover him, and then I won't be distracted." I broke the circle and placed a blanket over his body, gently as though he was still sleeping rather than empty. I had no idea whether he felt the cold or not, but it made me feel like I was doing something to help. It had been three days and we hadn't been able to find any spells that would bind Lionel's spirit back to his body.

At least he didn't look, or smell, like he was decomposing. "The spell you used on his body is holding well." I tried to touch his cheek, something I failed to resist doing daily. I couldn't make contact with his skin. There was something encasing him, probably the spell that slows time.

"For heaven's sake, Quinn, snap out of it." Dionne pulled the back of my shirt and dragged me back to the circle. "He'll be fine long enough for us to get it solved, but only if you help. I don't know enough magic to do this alone." She twisted her ponytail into a knot behind her neck and rubbed at her eyes. Even at her age, the stress was starting to take a toll.

I had to admit, she was right. This wasn't like it was with Cate. Lionel wasn't dead. "Okay, let's get this done." I wasn't going to let the hopelessness take over. "You know what we need to do? We'll take a break after this."

"We can keep working," she said. "We don't need to stop."

I knew too well the danger of doing magic when you are tired. Dionne was young. She might be able to go longer than me, but she was also inexperienced. "We'll take a break. There's no point burning ourselves out. We have time. Like you said, Lionel will be fine for a while."

"Quinn, I—"

"No. This time I mean it. Finish the preparation. Maybe this will be the time we get what we need." I gave her the look I remembered hating from my training days. The one that promised serious, but unspecified, repercussions for not obeying.

She nodded and closed the circle again. "Yeah, everyone we asked said the only answers would be found in the circle. They just didn't know what we were supposed to do in the circle. Too bad Fionuir couldn't tell us how she found the spells."

I laughed. "I'm not sure anyone would have gotten the answer out of her even if she could help us. Fionuir will do anything she can to punish me for imprisoning her." Well maybe punish was too soft a word.

Dionne sat across from me, and then tossed the candy and precious stones into the center. "Okay, what's next?"

I smoothed the dirt testing for any contamination. I didn't want any mystery voices or killing spells to surprise us. Nothing seemed to be lurking, and the magic was almost fully returned from the bedrock where I'd sent it for the social worker's inspection. That brought a memory from our last meeting with Ms. Metcalfe and her comment about Dionne's age. "Dionne, when is your birthday?"

"Uh, why?" She studied the packed dirt beneath her.

"How do you avoid answering my questions? The oath you took should make you answer."

She shrugged. "I was going to answer. I just wondered why? Maybe the oath is more patient than you are."

The oath wasn't sentient. "I want to know how long we need to worry that Ms. Metcalfe is going to drop by."

"Oh, yeah, it's in two months. I've already told Ms. M that I'll be leaving school when I turn eighteen."

I created a small circle between us, hoping it would contain any danger. "Aren't you close to graduation?"

"Who cares? I'll be able to learn magic full time. Lionel can help make a room for me upstairs, and we can be a real coven, or whatever we're called."

I looked up to see that she was focused on the candy wrappers. "It would be a waste for you to quit school."

She looked up at me. "But I get to move in here, right?"

I dreaded the thought of having two apprentices living with me, especially one who seemed to find loopholes in her oath so easily. "That's the usual arrangement."

Her smile was a contrast to the worry that had tightened her face. "Great. I can probably start moving some of my stuff in over the next couple of months."

I agreed. "But you are not moving in until you are free of the system."

She picked up the candy and tossed it between her hands. "Yeah. Now let's get to it. Who are we going to call?"

I figured Ranseed would be our best bet since he knew who Lionel was and maybe would care about him, at least as much as a spirit can care about anything. "Okay, this inner circle won't let anything out, but you can put things in. Place two of the candies there and call for Ranseed."

Dionne did as I instructed. At least when it came to magic, she was willing to obey. She whispered the spirit's name. "Will he come right away?"

I gestured for her to be silent. We listened for a few minutes and then a faint sound of rustling leaves came to us. "Remember your question. He is likely to try to get something more than the candy, or give you useless answers."

She nodded and called his name again. Suddenly the rustling noise changed to a roar of pain and then silence.

Dionne opened her mouth, but I held up my hand. If Ranseed was angry, we needed to be sure he was in the circle before asking questions. If he wasn't there, our questions would float through the spirit world, and that meant anyone could answer. The way our luck was running lately, it would probably be a killing demon. Or that voice.

"Why have I been summoned?" his voice came just before a little whirl of dust disturbed the earth. Ranseed rarely showed visual evidence of his presence. I'd always known him as a whirl of dust and a variety of noises. He always displayed his mood as sound, and by the choice this time, he was curious.

Dionne sat straighter and looked to me for direction. I nodded.

She leaned toward the center. "We have questions of a magical nature."

The dust changed shape and seemed to point at Dionne. "Who are you?"

"Quinn's apprentice." She kept her voice even and seemed calm. I was proud of her composure.

Rustling filled the circle before Ranseed croaked out, "Not Lionel, but something more than an apprentice."

"Yes, I am not Lionel." She smiled. I saw her take control of the urge to look at Lionel. She was right to do so. Ranseed might not show it, but he could see what was going on around the circle.

"What is your question?"

I tensed. We'd rehearsed how to ask the question, and if Dionne followed the plan, it would be fine. If she did her own thing... well I wasn't sure what would happen.

"We are looking for a spell to bring a body and spirit together." She was sticking with the plan.

After a long pause, Ranseed said, "There is one. What will you pay for it?"

She looked at me, and I motioned for her to continue. "What price do you want?"

He laughed. "These candies and four favors."

Dionne narrowed her eyes. "No, the candies and one favor."

"Three."

Dionne smiled. "Three candies and one favor. Agreed."

"No, that is not what I said."

"You said three. You didn't say what three. Now what is the spell?"

I was impressed. Dionne was almost as good at negotiating as a druid.

"This spell can be found in the library of Alexander at—"

"No, not the location, the spell."

"I cannot tell you the spell. It is too complex."

Dionne glanced at Lionel's body. "Where is this library?"

"Hmm, it is not so much where, as when. It is in Abyssinia. It was destroyed three thousand years ago."

"Then it is of no use to us. The deal is not valid." Her tone gave no room for him to argue.

"Why do you need this spell? Are you dealing in necromancy?" The dust whirled into a tight column.

I watched her body tighten as the words came out. "No. The spirit of a friend has been separated from his body. He is not dead."

Was Dionne worried about giving too much information? Or hiding pain about Lionel?

"You wish a spell to reunite the friend? Who is this friend?"

She looked at me. I shook my head. There was no need to give him any information on the hope he'd be able to help. If he had anything useful, he would have given it for the favor.

"It doesn't matter. Please leave so we can contact someone with more information."

Good move on her part. If Ranseed was holding back, a knock at his pride would loosen his tongue.

"Before I leave, I have a message for Lionel of the one name." Ranseed's voice was like a rattle of bones.

"Lionel is not available." Dionne was good at diverting questions. I started to see how she managed to get what she wanted from everyone.

"Hmm, it is curious that he is indisposed. I would tell him that there is rumor that his time is coming."

"I'll tell him." Dionne looked at me and shrugged. "Goodbye."

We cleared the circle.

"What the hell was that about?"

"Who knows? It's hard to say what Ranseed might know about Lionel's future." I glanced over at Lionel's body. "You did well."

She blushed. "Thanks. So, who should we call next?"

"No one. If Ranseed didn't know, then no one else will, or no one on that plane. Let's eat, we'll think of something else."

CHAPTER 2

Dionne lost the pale, drawn look as she finished the sandwich I'd made her. I felt ready to pour more of my energy into the circle. Maybe an older spirit, one I wouldn't normally summon, would give us answers. "We need to summon some other spirits."

She looked at me. "What do you mean? I thought Ranseed was our only chance." Along with the color returning to her face, there was a glimmer of hope.

"There are others, but I don't go after them often. The price they ask is usually too high to make any deal worthwhile."

"But if it will save Lionel..." she said.

"Yes, then the price will probably be worth it." I started to clear away the remnants of the meal. Dionne rose to help me. I could tell she still had something to say. It was odd that she didn't just blurt it out.

"Quinn," Dionne said with ill-concealed fear. "If we don't find the answer today, I can make arrangements to stay over. I don't have to go home."

"I know you want to help. I would give everything to get

Lionel back, but we can't make the mistake of risking your ability to practice."

She sighed. "Exactly, I should be here more often. I've told my foster parents that I need to study more, that I might have to stay overnight with a friend."

"No. You know we can't risk having Ms. Metcalfe come by. And you know she will. She seems determined to make a success story out of you."

"But—"

"No buts. Don't lie to your foster parents, or your teachers, or Ms. Metcalfe. While you are in foster care, you need to be extra careful."

"Fine, let's get back to it since I only have a few more hours."

I checked the clock. "You have six more hours. Leave the dishes," I said. She was right, even if she'd exaggerated. We didn't have all day. I needed her to help with the magic because it would drain me too fast. The chores could wait until Lionel was back with us.

My phone rang as she picked through the candy bowl for more spirit bait. I looked at the caller ID.

"Speak of the devil and the devil appears. Or in this case, the social worker." I braced myself and accepted the call. "Ms. Metcalfe, I'm surprised to hear from you on a Saturday."

"I wish I didn't have to work on the weekend, Mr. Larson. But some things simply don't fit into the normal work week."

I glanced at Dionne. She looked like she was waiting for the blade to fall on her neck. I would have to get the details from her, if Ms. Metcalfe didn't just tell me. I had to balance my need to keep the social worker away from the house with my need to get her off the phone. "What can I do to help you?"

"I'm sorry to say that Dionne's school work is suffering due to this job. In the short time she's worked for you, she has missed the deadline on three assignments."

I glared at Dionne, but couldn't blame her when I was the one who needed her. "I see." Whatever Ms. Metcalfe wanted, I wasn't going to offer an opinion. I was supposed to be Dionne's employer, and I imagined that the normal employer wouldn't be all that ready to get involved.

"I will need to review her work schedule with you. Are you available on Monday?"

I gritted my teeth and tried to think of an answer that would keep her away from us forever. I didn't think she would believe that Dionne had quit, and it was too easy to check. "My day is full. Can we make it later in the week?"

"It does need to be sooner rather than later. How is Tuesday?" She wasn't going to be deterred. "I'm afraid it is important. Perhaps it will be okay to email me her schedule for the next month before we meet."

I couldn't remember if Dionne was supposed to be here today, and I didn't have a schedule for her. There was only so much I could do to make this fake employment seem real. "I can do that on Monday, if that's acceptable?"

She agreed and gave me her email address. "I will need to meet with you, Mr. Larson. Dionne was on her way to university before she decided to take on this job. I would hate for her to lose that future."

I really wanted to tell her that I wasn't responsible for every problem in Dionne's life. That I had a life to save, and a prophecy to solve, and her need for petty details was getting in the way of far more important things. "I'm sure Dionne will refocus. If this job is really getting in the way of her future, I can always find someone else to do the work." Dionne's face went white at my words. I shook my head and a little color returned.

"Oh, I don't think it will come to that. She enjoys her work." There was a reluctance in Ms. Metcalfe's voice that surprised me. Why did she keep trying to interfere if she thought Dionne should keep the job?

This felt like a good place to end the call, before I got in too deep. "Okay, well, I hope you have some time to relax this weekend. I need to get back to work. No rest for me either." I waited until she hung up before I ended the call.

I turned to Dionne. "We need to get this sorted out."

She shrugged. "I'll put a schedule together that she'll be happy with."

Was I like that as a teenager? She didn't seem to have any grasp of the fact that her behavior had consequences, let alone any fear of consequences. Maybe it was the result of living amongst the humans. "No, we need to find a way to balance your lessons here with your lessons at school. What's going on? Do you need to spend more time on your school work?"

"No." She swallowed. "Okay. I was spending time with my friends. I can't just ignore them. I guess I lost track of the time I spent with them. I'll make up the assignments."

Frustrated, I clenched my fists to avoid escalating this into an argument. "Yes, you will. When we've got Lionel back, you'll spend half your time here on school work and half on magic. We cannot risk discovery."

"What about getting me ready for the prophecy?" I could hear the strain of trying to sound cool in her voice.

There was no way to fix this. No real answer while we were in the middle of getting Lionel back. There were too many things that were absolutely important right now. "It won't be for long. You'll be out of the system soon, and the prophecy can't be that urgent. I think we'd see some signs if it was, and you would have been contacted by the others." I realized that I was trusting that she would tell me if she had been contacted, and then I became uneasy at the thought that she was very good at hiding things from me. "You haven't heard from anyone, have you?"

She shook her head. "I would have told you. I wish I wasn't a foster child. Maybe if I wasn't in the system, it would be easier to do this."

I couldn't be angry at her trying one more tactic to get me on her side. It was true, but if she wasn't in the system, I wouldn't be her teacher. "If your parents had survived, they would have raised you as a witch. You wouldn't be my apprentice."

"Yeah, I guess." She sat up straight and gave me a smile. "No point in wishing for the past to change. Let's get Lionel back, and then we'll have more control of our time."

I could only hope she was right. I couldn't help but feel like we were never going to get back to normal. This state of emergency was lasting so long that I didn't really remember what it was like before. The feeling of impending crisis was becoming my normal mood. "Okay, we'll try some more risky things now. I will do the summonings. You need to be silent, no matter what happens."

"Why can't I help?" Disappointment tinged her words. She'd been expecting to do everything. I guessed I wasn't the only one who needed time to get used to the fact that I could see.

"Would you accept, just because I said you can't?"

She laughed. "Should I? Is that what a good apprentice would do? Is that how you plan to get me ready for the prophecy?"

"Sometimes it would be nice to have a compliant apprentice," I said, glad we were at the teasing point. "I will do the magic, because I'm going to tap into some deep old spirits. They are hard to reach and highly unpredictable. If they know you are there, they will try to influence you to take their side in some games of power you won't understand."

"How do you know I won't understand?" Her annoyance was clear. She thought it was because she was young.

"Because I don't understand them." I went to a cupboard and reached into the far corner, pulling out a black jar sealed with an inch of wax.

"Who are they?" She took the jar from me. "I thought I just managed a spirit. Isn't Ranseed old?" She was curious now. I worried that she would be curious enough that she'd go looking on her own. Most apprentices didn't have the power to get to these beings without a master. I worried that Dionne would have enough power, and that she wouldn't have enough wisdom to stay away.

I didn't want to pique her interest with a ban on trying the magic. For a change, I could be grateful that we had so many deadlines. I kept it to the facts. "Not this old. These spirits, well I call them that, but I'm not really sure what kind of being they are, they are more ancient than the elementals. They play dark games of power that sometimes reach these planes."

My ploy must have worked because her voice was casual as she asked, "How do you know them?"

I needed to end this conversation and get us back to the workshop. I opened my mouth to tell her exactly that, but before I could answer the room became icy cold. A wailing came from an invisible, distant pain. The desolation of the sound raised tears in Dionne's eyes and froze my heart.

"Quinn, I thought I was the most powerful being you knew," The Morrigan's voice scratched across my nerves.

QUINN'S WORLD IS OUT OF CONTROL. USE THE QR CODE TO grab your copy of Imbalance and watch his reality fly out of control.

FREE EBOOK

Claim your copy of Spells and Other Charms when you use the QR code to sign up for my newsletter and learn more about Quinn and Cate's past.

ALSO BY P A WILSON

For more books by P A Wilson

Use the QR code below or go to pawilson.ca

ABOUT THE AUTHOR

Perry Wilson is a Canadian author based in Vancouver, BC who has big ideas and an itch to tell stories. Having spent some time on university, a career, and life in general, she returned to writing in 2008 and hasn't looked back since (well, maybe a little, but only while parallel parking).

She is a member of the Vancouver Writers Social Group, The Royal City Literary Arts Society, and The Surrey Writing Workshop. Perry has self-published several novels. She writes the Madeline Journeys, a fantasy series about a high-powered lawyer who finds herself trapped in a magical world, the Quinn Larson Quests, which follows the adventures of a wizard named Quinn who must contend with volatile fae in the heart of Vancouver, and the Charity Deacon Investigations, a mystery thriller series about a private eye who tends to fall into serious trouble with her cases, and The Riverton Romances, a series based in a small town in Oregon, one of her favorite states. Her stand-alone novels are Breaking the Bonds, Closing the Circle, and The Dragon at The Edge of The Map.

For more information
www.pawilson.ca
pawilson@pawilson.ca

ACKNOWLEDGMENTS

People think that the process of writing is solitary. That's not the case for me. I have help from so many people it would be hard to acknowledge everyone, but I'll give it a try.

The support and inspiration I get from my writer's groups is incalculable. The Vancouver Writers Social Group opens my mind to other ways of telling a story. The Royal City Literary Arts Society gives me the opportunity to meet and share with other writers who have more knowledge than I do. The Other 11 Months group is where I learn about getting the words on the page. And my critique group who helps me find the best parts of the story I want to tell. Thanks to all of the members of these great groups.

Last of all, but definitely a huge part of the process, my beta readers. These are the people who love stories and are willing, and more than able, to tell me if my finished story is ready for you, my readers.